MAGGIE'S GRAVE

DAVID SODERGREN

ALSO BY DAVID SODERGREN

THE FORGOTTEN ISLAND

"A blood-drenched love letter to Lovecraft, handled with impressive authority and confidence."
James Fahy, author of *The Changeling* series

NIGHT SHOOT

"Night Shoot is wildly entertaining. If you're not laughing, you're scared out of your mind."
Sadie Hartmann, *Mother Horror*

DEAD GIRL BLUES

"It takes guts to write a book like this and nail it in the way Sodergren does."
Matt Redmon, *Night Worms*

Cover illustration by Trevor Henderson
Graphic design by Heather Sodergren

To mum and dad,
for letting me watch all those horror films.
See, I told you it would all pay off one day.

1

Maggie Wall watched through the thin slit of the window as the six men arrived on horseback.

They had come to kill her.

It was written in the lines of their faces, in their posture, in their collective silence. Groups of men riding together are never quiet — they laugh, they sneer, they brawl. But not these men. Their faces were grim, their expressions severe.

She was going to die today.

There would be no trial, no chance to defend herself. But what did that matter? The trials were a sham, a cruel mockery of justice. She had witnessed many herself.

Bind her wrists and ankles and throw her in the river. If she floats, she's a witch. If she drowns...she's innocent.

It was hopeless. One time, several years ago, she had ridden past the Laird's house late at night, pausing to listen to the screams of young women as their "confessions" were tortured out of them.

Justice, aye? There *was* no justice. Just men with a perverse pleasure in the destruction of women's bodies. Maggie noticed her hand was fidgeting, and she gripped the edge of the table to stop herself.

The horses whinnied as the riders dismounted, the steeds retreating fearfully as the men advanced on her meagre stone dwelling, ruddy hands twitching over the hilts of their swords.

She should have left days ago, when the rumours had begun to spread.

She's a witch, little Timmy Cochran had said, and that was all it took. Three words from the mouth of a wretched pubescent were enough to damn her. She was surprised they hadn't come sooner. People talked, and there was nothing more suspicious to small-town minds than a woman living alone.

What does she do up there all by herself?

Why hasn't she taken a husband?

So many questions, each more banal than the last.

A pot boiled atop a fire beside her, the kindling snapping and hissing as it burned in the small alcove cut into the stone wall.

My cauldron, she thought, and laughed miserably. It was *soup*. No leg of frog or eye of bat, just chicken and herbs. It smelled delicious, yet she knew she would never taste it.

The men approached, false bravado imprinted over their cautious faces.

'Careful, men,' one of them said. '*My Timmy saw her turn a man to ash before his very eyes. She's in league with the devil!*'

Maggie shook her head sadly. Lies. It was all lies. She had caught Timmy Cochran sneaking into her chicken coop with a devious glint in his eyes. As she chased him from her property, the runt had tripped and fallen. She had skelped his arse for his troubles.

Foolish.

This was why she kept to herself, grew her own vegetables, reared her own stock. This was why she had moved as far from other people as she could possibly manage.

'*There!*' cried another of the men. '*In the window!*' His pitch rose to a feverish delirium. '*The witch has seen us!*'

The way his façade cracked, Maggie thought he might piss himself in terror. On a different day, it may even have been funny.

'*Don't look directly at her! Steel your hearts, men, or she shall pluck them from your chests and devour them.*'

The men held their hands up to cover their faces as if squinting into the sunrise. Maggie abandoned her post at the window and scurried across the room to the front door, peering out. It seemed quiet. The wind howled through the trees, shaking branches and dislodging pine cones. She looked closer, at the bushes that rustled unnaturally, at the brief flashes of colour through the dried grass and heather, and knew she was surrounded.

'We mean you no quarrel, Maggie,' shouted Timmy Cochran's father in his Irish lilt. 'Come out and face trial.'

Maggie hurried back to the window.

'There'll be no trial, Cochran,' she said. 'You know as well as I.'

'That may be true, Maggie, and yet still I beseech you. Is it not better to die with dignity?'

Her fingers tightened, long nails gouging shallow troughs in the wooden table. The corners of her lips curled expectantly.

Cochran took a tentative step closer to the cottage and then disappeared from sight, the ground opening beneath his feet and welcoming him to its earthy bosom. He screamed in agony, and Maggie imagined the man at the bottom of the pit, impaled on the row of sharpened stakes that she herself had placed there.

She didn't mean to, but she laughed.

'*My God,*' shouted one of the men. '*The ground itself carries the witch's curse!*'

'*Be not afraid! We must stop this devilry! It's an affront to God!*'

Cochran's wails emanated from the bowels of the Earth. His would be a slow death, and an excruciating one. More men appeared from the forest that cocooned Maggie's cottage, Cochran having apparently brought all the menfolk in town. They continued onwards, stabbing at the ground in front of them with their sticks and swords like weary travellers.

She heard a faint creak and turned to see the door groaning open, a moon-faced man entering, eyes stricken with terror. Maggie recognised him as George MacKenzie, the butcher. His brow furrowed beneath the glistening bald dome of his head. Despite the icy wind that shrieked across the mountain, he was sweating.

'I am inside!' he cried, no doubt hoping the others would follow with haste.

'Look at me,' said Maggie, but he refused to meet her gaze. 'Look at me!'

'No, you foul, unearthly being,' he said through gritted teeth, averting his eyes. 'The children have seen you cavorting naked with the devil. It's unholy!' His sword swung loosely from his leather belt, and he reached for it with hands that trembled like a frightened hare.

The sword screeched as he unsheathed it, and Maggie grabbed the boiling pot from the alcove and rushed forwards, the metal searing her unprotected palms. Ignoring the pain that flared through her, she hurled the contents of the pot into MacKenzie's face. The liquid drenched the man, chunks of chicken slopping at his feet, and he brought both hands to his face with a roar of agony as steam rose from the bubbling mess. His rigid hands raked over his skin, globs of flesh dripping from his fingertips.

'Begone!' shouted Maggie. 'Or I shall curse you all!'

She had no choice but to play along. Maggie was no more a witch than the sun was a potato, but fear of her "powers" was her only chance of survival. It had worked before, years ago on the west coast, when she had bought herself enough time to escape. But today was different. Her hand shot instinctively to her swollen belly.

This time there were two of them.

She wondered if Malone was one of the men surrounding her cottage. It was *his* child she carried. She had found him drunk by the side of the road on one of her increasingly rare excursions into town, face down in the freezing mud. Fearful for his health, she had stuffed him in her cart alongside two squealing pigs and brought him back to her cottage. There, she had lain him in her cot, draped a blanket over him, and brewed an old remedy her mother had taught her, God rest her soul. The next morning Malone had risen, grateful for her assistance. They made love once, before he ventured home to his wife and four children.

It was the last she had seen of him.

A voice jolted her back to reality.

'Fear not, men! The light of our lord and saviour will guide us!'

'I renounce your pitiful god,' screamed Maggie, struggling to be heard over the cries of the faceless man writhing at her feet, his skin coming away in thick slices. She watched the butcher crawl blindly across the floor, his face a weeping scarlet horror, and felt sick to her stomach. Regardless of whether she had been defending herself or not, she had destroyed a man, robbed him of his face, his eyes, his livelihood. Shame seeped insidiously through her veins. She never wanted to hurt anyone...but why were they so intent on hurting *her*?

The door flew open and two men entered, crucifixes clutched in their hands. They rushed her, careful not to make eye contact, and dragged her to the ground.

'We have her! We have the witch!'

Maggie thrashed her limbs, but the men were too strong. More entered, crowding round her, until her cottage was fit to burst with the sheer amount of occupants. A cockerel crowed outside, the orange light of the morning sun muscling its way through the trees and into the cottage. The men formed a circle around her, a weapon in each of their hands.

'Pluck out her eyes!' screamed one of them, his face contorting madly as he spoke, spittle flying from his mouth. The others looked towards the man with the crucifix. He gripped it tightly, kissed it, and solemnly nodded.

Hands groped for her face, thick thumbs finding her eyeballs. She pressed her eyes shut, but the probing digits forced their way in, tearing through the thin membrane of her eyelids and exerting tremendous pressure until her eyeballs could take no more and popped inside her skull.

'The deed is done!'

Maggie tried to speak, to scream, to beg for mercy, but speech deserted her.

'*My God,*' a tremulous voice said. '*Look at her belly.*'

She recognised the voice. It was Malone.

'Strip her,' one of them said. 'Let us see what lies beneath her cunning disguise.'

Unseen hands went to work, clutching at her homemade dress, the stitches splitting as they tore it from her body, ripping it off and casting it aside. She lay naked before them, tears of viscous matter dribbling from the hollow craters of her ruined eyes. The men continued to talk, their voices blending into one hopeless cacophony.

'The fiend is with child!'

'It will be an abomination!'

'But what if the baby is innocent?'

There was a moment of silence. She imagined the minister holding his crucifix the way a child clings to a doll. Fury boiled within Maggie's breast. They could do what they wanted with her...but they dare not touch her baby.

They *dare* not.

'The child must face trial,' said the minister with dreadful certainty. 'Only God may judge the innocent.'

'But the witch cannot be allowed to live!' That was Malone again. The fear in his voice filled Maggie with a strange yet delicious sense of satisfaction.

'True,' said the minister. 'Then we must cut it out of her, free the abomination from the shackles of its mother's hellish womb.'

Maggie whipped her head back and forth in a frenzy, finding her voice once more. 'It's yours, Malone! This child is borne of your seed!'

'The creature lies!' said Malone. 'Is there no depth of depravity to which this witch will not sink?'

'It's yours! It's yours! It's yours!'

There came a sharp blow to Maggie's face, a vicious kick that broke her jaw, but she barely noticed. Her mind started to crumble, piece by piece. Soon, there would be nothing left. The men pinioned her arms to the ground, others unsheathing their weathered swords. They drove the blades into her open palms, and she welcomed the sweet relief of agony. Calloused hands parted her legs, and as the veil of madness descended, she let her body rest, awaiting the inevitable.

When she smiled, the men fell silent.

'A curse!' she said. 'A curse on you all. On this very town, and all who dwell within.'

'Where is the holy man? Bring him here!'

She laughed, a shrill, ungodly sound that caused more than one of the men to back away. *A curse! A blood curse on all your children!'*

'She admits it! The witch has confessed!'

'So be it, weak-minded fools!' she screamed. *'I give myself over to thee, Satan! I give thee my body and my soul!'*

Something penetrated her stomach, cold and sharp and deadly, and her lamentations turned to blood-soaked gurgles.

As Maggie faded, she heard something over the sounds of torn flesh and cracked bones. She thought it was a baby crying.

She smiled.

'A curse,' she whispered, and then Maggie Wall was no more.

2

Aside from drinking, fucking, and bowling, there wasn't a whole lot else to do on a Friday night in Auchenmullan. The town — if you could call it that — was dead, and had been for years, ever since the sawmill closed back in 2013. Once a small but thriving community in the Scottish Highlands, Auchenmullan was all but abandoned now, a ghost town, and forty-seven people were all that remained within its borders.

It sat in the shadow of a mountain, empty houses decomposing on deserted streets like toys outgrown by children, wildlife setting up home in the dank undergrowth of long-untended gardens. Some of the doors were unlocked, and in one place on Pine Street the TV was still on, two years after the MacDonalds had left for pastures new.

Even the electricity board had forgotten about Auchenmullan.

There was a church, and a small building that doubled

as a police station, its single cell unoccupied for over a year. No shops remained, Ian's Hardware and Electrical Store being the last to close its weary doors about six months back. No one saw Ian leave, or knew where he went, but that was the way of Auchenmullan these days. People just drifted away like fine grains of sand on an autumn breeze.

On this particular Friday night, town history was the last thing on Beth Collins' mind as she rested both hands on the jukebox of Spring-heeled Jack's Tenpin Bowling Alley. She slammed in fifty pence and perused the selection of songs, flipping through the racks as if somehow she would find a new record on there. She knew she wouldn't. The jukebox — like the paint and decor — hadn't been updated since the alley had opened before she was born.

She flipped past *Don't Stop Believing*, which had been playing when she took her first sip of alcohol in this very room, and flipped some more. *Be My Baby*. She had lost her virginity to Grady Cooper to that song four years ago, up against the door of the last cubicle in the women's toilet. He hadn't even lasted the two-and-a-half minutes of the song, but neither of them had cared. She looked over at him now, in his faded Pearl Jam shirt and long hair — which was in danger of becoming a mullet — goofing off in front of their friends, or what remained of them.

Four teenagers. The youth of Auchenmullan.

Four desperate, lonely teenagers.

There had been talk of building a school once, before the fire destroyed the mill and, with it, the livelihoods of the residents. Things could have been so different.

'Choose a song, Beth!' shouted Grady, and she responded with a half-hearted thumbs-up. She hadn't noticed the silence. In Auchenmullan, you got used to it.

You had to.

She selected *Leave A Light On For Me* by Belinda Carlisle. Behind the counter, Spring-heeled Jack himself polished unused beer glasses, looking as tired as Beth felt. How long had he worked here, how long had he owned this place? Did old Jack have dreams too, dreams that were crushed along with the rest of the town? The alley used to really rock on the weekends, kids and adults mingling together and having fun, but now the bowling alley was the last remaining business in Auchenmullan, and the four of them had free run of the place. Jack sold beer and basic groceries alongside the moth-eaten bowling shoes, and the condom machine in the men's room was always well stocked, but anything fancier was a thirty-seven mile ride into Inverness.

No wonder Grady's hair is getting out of control, she thought idly. *I should cut it myself before he reaches peak mullet.*

She watched Jack hobble from behind the counter to collect her friends' discarded bottles and wondered how he'd ever been given the nickname Spring-heeled Jack. Was it meant to be ironic? She supposed he too had been young, once. Would that be her in forty years' time? Is this what she had to look forward to, rotting away in Auchenmullan like a corpse in the ground?

Like Maggie Wall...

Beth paused.

That was weird. She hadn't thought of Maggie Wall in years. Her grandpa used to spook her and her best friend Alice by telling them the legend of Maggie around the campfire near Cook's Point, high on the mountain.

In Auchenmullan, it was a rite of passage.

But her grandpa had been dead for almost a decade. She had been nine or ten then, and now she was fast approaching her twenties. Funny how Maggie Wall should come back into her thoughts like that. Perhaps she was becoming a true Auchenmullaner, and one day, she and Grady would take their children's children camping up there, on top of the mountain, and retell the old legend before passing away themselves, forgotten and unloved. What would be left of the town in fifty years? Beth sometimes thought it would be for the best if the ground would just open up and swallow the whole damn place.

Things were so much simpler when she was younger. Her parents had made all her decisions for her, and she didn't have the constant threat of adulthood hovering over her shoulder.

Beth abandoned the jukebox and strolled behind the counter, grabbing two cans of Tennents from the fridge and leaving a crumpled note on the register. Jack saw her, grunted, and went back to whatever the hell he was doing.

She handed one of the beers to Grady. He kissed her on the cheek and took a drink.

He looks older, she thought. *And not in a good way.*

Beth didn't mean it unkindly. She loved Grady, or at least she had, once. Now she wasn't so sure. The town was ageing them prematurely, a decrepit vampire sucking their lifeforce with each dreary, wasteful day.

She noticed Grady was talking to her.

'What?' she said.

'You okay?'

'Just thinking.'

'About what?'

'Maggie Wall,' she said. She expected Grady to laugh at her, but he didn't.

'Huh,' was all he said.

'Yeah.'

She sipped her beer. Interactions like this were increasingly common. There was only so much you could say to the same people every day before staleness set in.

Grady looked toward the lanes, where Steve and Alice were waving impatiently at them. 'Guess we'd better get back to the game,' he said.

'Yeah. Good talking to you.'

Grady shook his head. 'Don't start. Not tonight.'

She looked at him and tried to dredge up the old feelings. Did she still love him? He was the same boyishly handsome idiot she had fallen for all those years ago — in that respect, he hadn't changed. But maybe that was the problem? And anyway, what would happen if they broke up? They would still see each other every fucking day. It was unavoidable.

God, she hated this stupid little town.

'Be-eth, it's your turn,' shouted Steve, cupping his hands around his mouth, his burly frame packed into a too-small jeans and shirt combo, his once muscular stomach creeping over the top of his belt. He sounded annoyed, but Steve always sounded that way. It's just who he was. In other circumstances, they would never have been friends, but when you're one of only four teenagers in town, you learn to tolerate people.

Even the arseholes.

Beth handed Grady her beer and bowled two gutter balls in a row. She didn't care. She hated bowling. They all did. But the alley was the only place in town to buy alcohol, and Jack only served you if you were playing. A businessman to the end, old Jack, the crafty devil.

As usual, Steve cackled at Beth's lack of bowling skills and, as usual, she ignored him. She sidled up next to her oldest friend, Alice Burman, and sat by her. Like Grady,

Alice needed a haircut. She looked tired, but at least Alice had an excuse for that.

'How you feeling?' said Beth.

Alice raised her beer in acknowledgement. 'Good to taste this again. You don't know how hard it is to live here and not get drunk for nine months.'

'I can't even imagine.'

Alice looked adoringly at her bottle of Peroni. 'This shit makes life bearable.'

'You're drunk,' said Beth.

'This is my first one,' said Alice. 'How about you?'

'I've lost count.' She checked her watch. It wasn't even six.

Better pace yourself, or you'll be in bed by eight.

Would that be so bad? How many Friday nights had she — had all of them — wiled away under the leaking roof of the bowling alley, listening to power ballads and the steady rattle of the heating, wishing something — anything — would happen? How many more, until she could sever ties with this dead-end place and move on with her life? She had ambitions. A talented artist, she always figured she would go to university.

You're the best artist in Auchenmullan, but that means nothing. Think you could cut it with the best the rest of the world has to offer?

She drank, sipping her beer and burping. Grady stole a look at her and she smiled.

Everything is fine. We were born here, and we'll die here, and life will move on without us. Everything is hunky-dory. We're the forgotten kids of Auchenmullan!

She turned her attention back to Alice. 'Seriously though, how are you? Is motherhood all you dreamt it would be?'

'It is. It's just as shitty as I feared.'

'You look good,' said Beth. Another lie. They came to her too easily these days.

Alice pointed at the dark bags under her eyes. 'You too could look this good on three hours sleep. I mean, I love the little guy, but last night I was up every hour to feed him. You should see the state of my nipples,' she laughed.

'What's that?' shouted Steve. Steve shouted a lot. For him, silence was an inconvenience. He grinned. 'Is someone talking about nipples?'

'Dry, cracked and sore,' said Alice, and Steve made a disgusted face and turned away.

Beth didn't know what else to say, which was odd, because she and Alice had been friends since nursery. But now her best friend was a *mother*, and Beth couldn't help but feel the dynamic between them had shifted. Alice was officially a grown-up, even though she didn't always act like one. The father, a spotty kid named Kevin, left one week after finding out about the baby, his parents abandoning the house unsold and seeking a new life elsewhere, which seemed a bit of an overreaction. So far, Alice's attempts to track Kevin down had been unsuccessful, and as the town had little internet connection due to the surrounding mountains, it looked like remaining that way for some time.

'At least your mum is there to help,' said Beth, sensing the awkwardness between them. Were *they* growing apart too? First Grady, then Alice. Pretty soon her only friend would be Steve, and she didn't even like him.

Alice smiled sadly. 'I guess so. You should come round and see Eric sometime. Oh, I forgot to tell you, he laughed! It was so cute, he...Beth, are you listening?'

'Huh? Oh, yeah, sorry. Guess I've got a lot on my mind just now.'

'The fast pace of life in Auchenmullan too much for you?'

'Something like that, yeah.'

'It's Grady, isn't it?'

Beth bit her lip. 'You know me too well.'

'Wanna talk about it?'

Beth shrugged. She did and she didn't, because if she *did*, she worried that whatever she said could also apply to Alice.

'It's this town,' she said instead. 'I hate it. You really want to bring Eric up in a place like this?'

'Don't have much choice, do I?' said Alice. Beth thought she did have a choice, but once again chose to say nothing. It was better to avoid unnecessary arguments. Just keep everything civil. Get along with everyone. Pass the time.

What else was there to do?

Alice was drunk by the time ten o'clock rolled around. All of them were, but Alice had only had two beers. She hiccuped softly to herself. Those beers were the first drops of alcohol she'd had since finding out she was pregnant, and while she enjoyed them, she felt that two were sufficient.

She wanted to get home to Eric.

This was the first time they had been apart since the birth. It was only for five hours, but it felt like forever. Oh sure, it had been great to see her friends, but being apart from him caused her heart to ache. It was a new sensation, and one she wondered if she would ever get used to. Once he was a little older, she could bring him along to the alley. Maybe *then* Beth would spend some time with him.

Come on, that's the booze talking.

But it wasn't. It was the truth, and she knew it. Even

tonight, when she had tried to engage her in conversation about Eric, the topic had quickly reverted to Beth's problems with Grady. Alice never wanted to become one of those tiresome parents who spoke about nothing but their kids, but she hoped — no, *expected* — her best friend to show even the tiniest morsel of interest.

Forget it. Give her time. Get back to Eric.

That was the plan. A short walk to clear her head, and then home. She had expressed some milk that morning with her new electric pump so her mum could feed him. It felt wrong having someone else do it, though. That was *her* job.

Christ, she missed the little guy. Missed him like hell. She didn't care that his life was currently a cycle of eating, sleeping, crying and shitting.

He'll fit in just fine in Auchenmullan, she thought. It sounded like something Beth would say.

'Closing time,' bellowed Spring-heeled Jack. The bowling had finished two hours ago, and they were sitting by the lane nursing the dregs of their pints.

'Just finishing up,' said Steve.

'Fuck off,' said Jack, and Steve laughed.

Alice smiled. She hadn't been to Jack's for months, but nothing had changed, and she was thankful for that. Whether Beth liked it or not, Alice's entire life had radically altered with the arrival of Eric, and she was glad to find a sense of routine between the four walls of the alley. It made her feel like everything was going to be alright.

They grabbed their jackets and headed out the door, converging in the parking lot. It was chilly out, the sky dark with thunderous clouds, and Alice rubbed her hands together for warmth, wishing she'd brought gloves. Only two vehicles sat in the lot, Jack's red Fiat and Steve's van.

'Hey Al, need a lift?' said Steve, trying not to appear cold as he shivered in a thin blue sweater.

She shook her head. 'Nah, think I'm gonna walk the beers off.'

'What about you guys?' he asked Beth and Grady, but they were already heading out of the lot and down the street. He gave Alice a look, and she raised her eyebrows.

'What's up with them?' she said.

'What do you mean?'

Alice couldn't figure out if he was joking. 'Have you not noticed anything different about Beth lately?'

'Nope. Well, last month I thought she'd had a boob job, but she was just wearing a new bra.'

Alice sighed. 'Good night, Steve,' she said, turning to leave.

'Hey, wait a minute.'

She stopped and looked at him.

Steve stuck his hands in his pockets and shuffled on his feet. 'It's good to have you back,' he said, embarrassment creeping into his face. 'It's boring being the third wheel every night.'

'It's good to *be* back. I missed you guys.'

'I missed you too. I mean, *we* missed you.' He looked down at the ground. 'How's the kid?'

'He's fine, Steve,' she said, then added, 'Thanks for asking.'

It felt nice to have someone show an interest.

'I'll need to come round and see him.' He laughed. 'My mum wants a picture of him.'

'You do that. I think you'd like him. He's probably your intellectual equal.'

'You mean that?' grinned Steve, and once again, Alice wasn't sure if he was kidding or not.

'How about tonight?' he said. 'Or if, uh, you want to stay out a little longer, I have more beers in the van.'

'I bet you do,' she said dryly.

Even in the dark, she could see his face colouring. 'It's just...remember that night a while back? Before Christmas? I had fun. I was thinking we could—'

'I remember, Steve. And I enjoyed it too.'

Steve grinned that rarest of grins, the sincere Steve smile, and she remembered that when he wasn't being an arsehole, he could be a sweet guy.

'So you wanna...'

She held up a hand to stop him. 'Not tonight, pal. I have to get home.'

He nodded. 'Aye, no problem. Sorry, I've had a few drinks, y'know.'

It was amusing to see Steve like this, but she decided to put him out of his misery.

'Don't forget,' she said, 'I just pushed a *baby* out of there.'

Steve's face lit up. 'Well, maybe this time I'll be able to fit my massive—'

'Aaaaand he's back,' laughed Alice. 'You can't help yourself, can you?'

He shrugged. 'Sorry. It's just that I like you...'

'Night, Steve,' she said. She started to go, then walked up to him and kissed him on the cheek.

'Night,' he said. 'You get home alright?'

'I'll be fine. Why are you worrying?' She glanced involuntarily at the mountain that loomed above them, unsure why. When she looked back, she noticed Steve was doing the same.

'I dunno,' he said. 'There's a...funny feeling in the air. Ah shite, that sounds daft.'

'No, I feel it too. It's like...'

But she didn't have the words. She *couldn't* explain it. At first she thought it was anxiety at leaving the house, at leaving Eric alone, but it was more than that.

'Be careful,' said Steve, and she almost laughed until she saw the worry on his face.

She touched his arm. 'I will.'

Steve clambered into the van, gunned the engine, and blared the horn as he drove off down the streets, weaving drunkenly across the empty road.

Alice took a last nervous glance up towards the mountain, then started her walk home. She pulled her coat tighter across her chest, her breath fogging before her, wishing she'd let Steve drive her.

He was right.

There was something in the air tonight, and she didn't like it one bit.

3

THE SKY THREATENED RAIN.

Beth pulled her beanie hat down over her ears, wondering if it would soon be cold enough for snow. Part of her hoped it would. At least then she and Grady would have something to talk about. He walked beside her, scuffing his feet along the pavement. She knew what that meant. He was in a mood, angry with her for some unknown reason. God, he could be so childish.

'You could have said goodbye to them,' he said. 'You've hardly seen Alice since she had the baby.'

Beth balled her fists in frustration. Lately, everything Grady said or did made her mad. Especially when it was truthful.

'I just want to get home. I'm tired.'

'And drunk,' he muttered.

They continued down the deserted street. Far above them the moon kept watch between the quickly amassing clouds, alighting the old playground as they strolled unhurriedly past. The grass was as high as the swings now, and though it was dark, the rusted discolouration of the metal was visible. The slide lay on its side, hidden by the weeds, though the steps leading up to it remained, a stairway to nowhere. Was that a metaphor? Beth was too tired, too drunk, to know.

They rounded the corner onto Gordon Street in silence. One family still lived here, the Krauses, but their lights were off. Dave and Mary Kraus were in their seventies, and probably in bed.

'This place is dead,' whispered Beth.

'It could be worse,' said Grady, though he didn't elaborate on how that would be possible. They walked on, passing a field of cows. The beasts seemed to watch them, their eyes dull with judgement, tails swinging languorously.

'Hey, remember that time we went cow-tipping?' said Grady, and Beth smiled.

'It almost fell on top of Steve,' she said.

Grady chuckled. 'It was his fault for standing on the wrong side.'

The memory quickly faded. She knew what Grady was trying to do. Make her think about the old days, about the fun they used to have. But there was only so far nostalgia could take you.

Something up ahead caught her eye.

It was a man. He stood in the middle of the road, cloaked in heavy shadow.

'Why do you hate this place so much?' said Grady, but she wasn't listening.

She watched the man standing there, unmoving, his body turned towards the mountain. A car was parked nearby, its white paintwork glowing in the moonlight. A police car.

'I mean, is it me?' continued Grady. 'Are you fed up with me?'

'Quiet,' she said, stopping, holding up an arm to block him.

'What now?'

'Over there,' she said, gesturing towards the man. 'Who is that?'

Grady squinted. 'Looks like Larry.' He pointed at the police vehicle. 'That's his car.'

'What's he doing?'

'Beth, were you listening to me? I asked if—'

'What's he *looking* at?' she said, more insistently this time.

Grady shook his head. 'Fine, ignore me.'

She exhaled angrily. 'Look, I just want to know what he's doing in the middle of the street at half ten.'

'Why don't you ask him?'

The Larry that Grady referred to was Inspector Lawrence Carlisle, the last remaining police officer in Auchenmullan, arguably the easiest job in the world. As far as cops went, Beth thought he was at least bearable, despite his penchant for dumb catchphrases, the worst being, *'I put the Law in Lawrence.'* Most of the townsfolk simply addressed him as Larry, but he insisted that Beth, Grady, Steve, and Alice called him Inspector.

Typical cop power-trip.

'Hey, Inspector,' shouted Grady. The man did not respond, didn't even seem to hear them.

'You sure it's him?' said Beth. Without realising it, she huddled closer to Grady.

'Yeah...I think so. Come on.'

Grady started forward, practically dragging Beth with him by the arm. She wanted to dig her heels in. Something about this felt wrong.

'Inspector,' said Grady. 'Hey, Carlisle, is that you?'

Still no response. He just stood there, staring off into space. Beth followed his gaze to the mountain. She could identify Cook's Point, and Maggie Wall once more crept into her thoughts like the roots of a tree pushing through the soil.

What the hell is it with Maggie Wall today?

'Hey Larry,' said Grady, and the man finally acknowledged them.

'Oh...evening,' said Carlisle. He was a broad man, mid-fifties, with a full head of blonde hair that he had recently had cut after someone told him he resembled Donald Trump.

'You okay, sir?' said Beth.

Carlisle looked confused, almost as if he didn't know where he was. 'You lot wrapped up early tonight, eh?' he said, trying to sound conversational.

'It's half-ten,' said Grady.

'Oh, uh...yeah.'

'What are you looking at?' said Beth.

Carlisle snapped his gaze away from the mountain and faced her. 'Nothing,' he said. 'Nothing at all. How's Alice?' His eyes briefly betrayed him, flicking back to Cook's Point.

'She's fine,' said Beth.

'And the wean?'

'Eric? He's fine too.'

Carlisle nodded. 'Good. That's good. We're all fine.'

The temperature was plummeting rapidly. Beth nudged Grady, and they exchanged a glance.

'I guess we'd better be on our way,' said Beth. Carlisle said nothing. They walked past him. The streets ahead were dark, and though Beth knew them like the back of her hand, they were different tonight. Unreal, somehow.

'Hey,' said Carlisle as they made their escape. They

turned to look at him, but he just stared out over the hills and fields towards the mountain. 'Watch yourself out there,' he said.

'We will,' said Grady, but Beth doubted Carlisle was listening.

'Come on,' she said. She no longer felt drunk.

Just very uneasy.

'Slow down,' said Grady, and Beth realised she was close to breaking out into a jog. Her heart hammered in her chest for reasons she couldn't pinpoint. Despite passing them every day for the last few years, the abandoned houses seemed to take on a sinister aspect. The trees swayed, their movements lifelike, almost human.

'I want to go home,' said Beth. She felt short of breath and loosened her scarf.

'Okay, but we don't need to run. We're almost at my place,' said Grady, struggling to keep up. Neither of them spoke again until they arrived at the two-storey detached property where Grady lived with his parents, and only then did Beth slow her pace.

'What's gotten into you?' asked Grady. He reached for her hand, but she pulled it away.

'I don't know. Something doesn't feel right.'

'You had six pints tonight. It's probably your liver.'

'Why do you care about how much I drink? There's nothing else to do here.'

Grady dropped his gaze. 'Let's not do this again. Please. Why don't you come in, spend the night?'

The wind whistled through the birch trees that lined the streets. It was a noise Beth was intimately familiar with, and yet tonight the ghostly sound set her on edge. There was no reason for it. No reason at all.

'No, I'm going home,' she said.

Grady nodded as if he had been expecting her to say precisely that. 'Want me to walk with you?'

'I'll be okay.'

He leaned in to kiss her and she stepped back.

'What the fuck?' said Grady. 'I can't even kiss you goodnight?'

'I don't feel well.'

'Fine, go home. Go hide in your room. Have another drink while you're at it.'

'Maybe I will,' she said, whirling away from him and walking into the wind. The breeze blew her dark hair across her face, and she angrily brushed it aside.

'You're not a wee girl anymore,' shouted Grady.

Keep your fucking voice down, she thought, and then realised there was no one around to hear him anyway. Grady's family were the only ones living on the street. Like most people in town, they had the whole row of houses to themselves. She stormed away, Grady following behind her, his footsteps echoing through the night. She kept her head down, ignoring him, not letting him catch up. What the hell did he want? There was nothing left to be said.

He was gaining on her, the steps getting louder, faster, matching her heartbeat. She looked down at her feet, but the drunkenness returned and she felt herself sway.

'Fuck off and leave me alone,' she said, refusing to look at him, refusing to give him the satisfaction. What did he think, that she was going to stop, and he would catch up to her and kiss her, and it would start to rain like in some dumb Hollywood movie, and everything would be alright again?

Bullshit. Everything was wrong, everything was fucked up. They were stuck here, atrophying in the gloom of the mountain, the world moving on and leaving them behind.

Grady was almost level with her, and Beth sped up. Liquid slopped around inside her stomach. Grady was right about one thing — she *was* drinking too much these days.

She felt Grady's hand on her shoulder and spun to face him.

'Would you just leave—'

But there was no one there.

The street was quiet, barren, nothing moving except the trees and an empty Coke can rolling in the wind. But how could that be? Someone had grabbed her shoulder. Her gaze darted to the nearest bushes, but they were too far away. Someone had been following her...she had heard the steps all the way from Grady's house. But where were they now? It wasn't the booze. It couldn't be.

Beth glanced over the tops of the houses, up towards Cook's Point. The black outline of the mountain was almost invisible against the navy sky. She stood a moment, watching, and wondered once more what Carlisle had been looking at. From the other end of town, Evelyn Ronald's golden retriever started barking. Every night for the last two weeks the poor dog had been howling at the moon.

What does he know? she thought, and then the breeze picked up, shaking the branches of the trees like so many bony arms.

Beth turned away from Cook's Point, put her head down, and ran all the way home.

4

ON THE OPPOSITE SIDE OF TOWN, ALICE BURMAN APPROACHED her house, listening to the plaintive howl of Evelyn's dog echo across the neighbourhood.

That better stop soon, she thought. The windows in her room were not double-glazed, and she could hear everything through them, from rain hitting the recycling bin to the high-pitched calls of the osprey that nested nearby. It wasn't the dog's fault something had spooked him, but it better not keep her or Eric awake. Sleep was hard enough to come by these days.

The front door was unlocked, and she stepped inside, squeezing past the second-hand pushchair that now lived at the bottom of the hall stairs. No one in Auchenmullan locked their doors, because why would they? They knew everyone in town, and the only tourists that passed through were those who had taken a wrong turn on their way to Loch Ness.

The hall light was on, the TV playing faintly from behind the living room door. Alice kicked her shoes off and crept through the hall. Her mother was asleep in front of the television, a rerun of *Bullseye* on the screen. The baby monitor sat next to an empty glass of wine on the coffee table, the tinny receiver emitting its usual hum of static. She heard Eric gurgle through the monitor, and smiled to herself. It was nice to get out and see her friends, but all she wanted was to snuggle up in bed near her son.

Her son.

It was so crazy. She had always wanted children, but hadn't planned on it until she hit thirty. Now she was a teen mum, the kind who appears on *The Jeremy Kyle Show* to boos and jeers from the audience.

This here is Alice from the Scottish Highlands, she heard Jezza saying. *She's a single mum...who still lives with her mother...and she's only nineteen.*

She imagined the crowd gasping in horror, and stifled a giggle. So things hadn't gone exactly as planned...so what? For the first time in a long time, she felt truly happy.

Her mother groaned and shuffled into a more comfortable position on the sofa. Alice took the throw from the easy chair and draped it over her slumbering body, then switched the TV off. She turned the volume dial on the baby monitor until the crackle faded to nothing. The silence was palpable. Years back, the streets would have been alive with the thrum of traffic and young folk heading to The Vault, Auchenmullan's long-since departed nightclub. Now, the chances were high that she was the only person still awake, unless Beth and Grady had made up and gone to bed together. She doubted it. Something about her friend had changed, and she felt partly, irrationally responsible for it.

She switched off the light, listening for a moment to the low snores of her mother, and walked into the hall. Her room was at the top of the stairs.

It's Eric's room too, now.

Of course it was. They would share it for the first six months, which she hoped would give her time to sort out the spare room and convert it into a nursery. Maybe Beth could come round to help, and they could gossip and have a drink and a laugh, just like old times. Or was that a pipe dream? Did Beth even want to be friends with her anymore? They had only seen each other a handful of times since Eric's arrival. Sure, she hadn't been out to the bowling alley until tonight, but that was no excuse for Beth not to visit.

The staircase seemed to go on forever, and she realised how tired she truly was. Normally she was in bed by eight, and then Eric would wake her at ten, twelve, two...

A step creaked noisily beneath her feet, and Alice winced, expecting to hear his cries. Silence. Perhaps she would get a full night's sleep after all? He must be fast asleep. Dead to the world.

Don't say that.

Panic suddenly gripped her, a fear unlike anything she had experienced before, an utter, inconceivable dread. She ran up the rest of the staircase, taking two steps at a time, not caring if she woke her mum.

It's fine, it's fine, she kept telling herself, though she didn't believe it.

Something was wrong with her baby.

Her sweating hands struggled with the brass door knob, and then she burst into the room and raced to the bedside crib.

Eric was there, his little chest rising and falling with each delicate breath. She reached out her trembling hand and his chubby fingers closed over her pinky. Tears came to her eyes, and she wept silently, overwhelmed with a mixture of terror and joy. Was this parenthood? Love and fear combined into one tiny ball of unimaginable stress?

Probably.

'Fuck it,' she whispered, and wiped a tear from her cheek. She looked guiltily at the monitor, worried her mother had heard her swear over it, then remembered she had switched the receiver off. She tried to imagine Eric when he was older, attempting to hide his profanity from her, and swore that she would always remember this moment, and not get mad when she heard him say *fuck* or *shit* or *damn*. Just not the really bad word, the one she didn't like to use. If he used *that* word, she'd—

Tap tap tap.

Alice's blood turned to ice.

Someone was tapping on the window. Someone was outside.

Alice looked up from Eric. They were on the second floor. There couldn't possibly be someone out there...

Tap...tap...

She slowly turned towards the window, afraid, but not as afraid as she had been moments before.

It was the birch tree in the yard, the branches blowing in the wind and knocking against the glass. That was something else she was going to do in the next month. Chop that damn tree down. It had spooked her as a kid, and it still had the capacity to freak her out as an adult. She wandered over and raised the window, grabbing the rogue branch and snapping it off, letting it fall to the grass below. Quietly, so as not to wake Eric, she lowered the window, and that's when she saw it, reflected in the glass.

The person in the room with her.

It wasn't a person though, not really. It didn't look human. The creature was too thin, too misshapen, so tall it hunched over at the waist, its skin grey and flaking. It looked up at Alice for a brief second, as if to make sure she was watching, and then its dreadful hands were reaching into the crib, reaching for her baby.

'Stop!' she screamed, her stomach lurching. She spun away from the window, drawing on vast reserves of courage she didn't know she possessed, coming face-to-face with...

Nothing.

There was nothing there.

A strange, inhuman noise filled the room, and it took her a second to realise it was Eric. He was awake, and crying. Alice tried to go to him, but her feet were immobile. She couldn't remember the last time her heart had taken a beat. The bedroom door burst open and Alice screamed again.

'Alice,' her mother said. 'What's going on?'

Her strength came to her gradually, filtering through her veins. She went to Eric, lifted him, cradled him, and perched unsteadily on the edge of the bed.

'My heavens, you look awful,' her mum said. She placed the back of her hand against Alice's forehead. 'You have a temperature.'

'I'm fine,' she said. What else could she say? That there was something in here? That it was trying to take her baby? She smiled unconvincingly at her mother, hoping the lie wouldn't show in the dim light of the bedroom. 'Honestly, I'm just tired.'

'You're not telling the truth. A mum can always tell. You'll learn that in time.'

'Yeah, okay,' said Alice, trying to laugh and failing. 'Go to bed. You sound like a fortune cookie.'

Her mother kissed her on the head. 'If you need me, wake me up,' she said, heading stiffly for the door, her dressing gown sashaying across the carpet. She paused in the doorway.

'You didn't...*see* anything, did you?' she asked falteringly. There was something unusual about the way she spoke.

'No,' said Alice. 'I just need a good rest.'

'That's right,' her mother said, as she closed the door. 'A good rest. That's what we all need.'

Eric lay in Alice's arms, snug and cosy, while she entertained absurd worries like was it possible to love someone too much, anything to stop thinking about what she had seen. She couldn't tell anyone. They would think she was insane, that she wasn't coping with the demands of motherhood. They would take Eric away from her.

She looked around the room that she had slept in for eighteen years and hardly recognised it. Her bed had been pushed up to the wall to make room for the crib, and a new dresser and changing station took up the remaining space. The flattened cardboard box from the car seat had been shoved behind the dresser where it would doubtlessly remain for the next thousand years.

The mess is only gonna get worse, she thought. *Just wait til his granny starts buying him toys.*

She smiled, and laid Eric down gently, taking her bra off beneath her jumper and removing her contact lenses in preparation for bed. Already she was beginning to question whether she had seen anything.

She was tired, that was all. Tired and a little tipsy.

Her eyelids were heavy, and she struggled to keep them up. She unzipped Eric's sleeping bag, checked his nappy, and kissed him goodnight.

Tap...tap...tap...

Something else was knocking at the window.

Another branch, that's all.

Yes, that was it. She told herself there was no point in checking. With her back to the window, Alice slipped off her jeans and climbed into bed, pulling the duvet up over her head. She *knew* there was nothing out there. But still, there was no sense risking it.

Tap...tap...tap...

She closed her eyes and tried to sleep, and after a while she did. Eric dozed most of the night, not waking her until four in the morning, and when she did wake, she felt good.

The strange creature in the room was a distant memory, and by midday Saturday, she had forgotten all about it.

5

BETH AWOKE WITH A STINGING HEADACHE, GOLDEN LIGHT streaming through the gauzy curtains of her bedroom. She closed her eyes, buried her face in the pillow, but it was too bright to continue sleeping.

Another hangover.

She tried to recall her argument with Grady last night, yet all she could think of was Carlisle standing alone in the middle of the road, the feeling of being followed home, and the phantom hand on her shoulder.

Bacon sizzled downstairs. The smell reached her nostrils, and her stomach grumbled angrily, ready to play its favourite game.

Hungry...or sick?

It was a fifty-fifty, but Beth knew where to place her bet. She slithered out of bed and marched to the bathroom in her loose-fitting tartan pyjamas. There, she hugged the toilet until she threw up, hoping the noise of the fry-up downstairs masked the cacophony of sounds erupting from her throat.

Did she have a problem? Grady thought so. He claimed

she was developing a dependancy on alcohol to get her through the day, and guess what? For once he was correct.

Even a broken clock is right twice a day.

'Beth, you up?' It was her father, calling from the kitchen. 'I'm making breakfast.'

That explained the strong smell of burning.

'I'll be down in a minute,' she shouted, forcing herself up, avoiding her own reflection in the mirror above the sink. There was no sense in making herself feel worse than she already did. She could imagine the drawn, pale face without having to see it, thank you very much.

She dressed in leggings and a baggy jumper, and headed downstairs, spraying copious amounts of perfume in place of a shower. Her mother was in the hallway, talking on the phone in a low, conspiratorial voice.

'Tonight?' she whispered. *'We can't...we just can't.'*

She sounded upset, and Beth waited out of sight, listening.

'I know, I've felt it too. We all have. But how? We did everything right...we did everything right. Okay...yes...yes...we'll be there. But I pray to God you're wrong.'

She hung up, and Beth made her way down the remaining stairs, gripping the bannister to steady herself.

'Who was that?' she said, and her mother shot her a nervous glance like a child caught with her hand in the biscuit jar.

'Nothing,' she said too quickly. 'I didn't hear you come home last night.'

'Changing the subject, nice try,' said Beth. 'But really... who was on the phone?'

'Larry Carlisle. There's a town meeting tonight. Your father and I will be attending.'

As if on cue, there came a cry of, *'Bacon's ready,'* from the kitchen, followed by, *'Oooh shit, that's hot!'*

'Am I invited?' asked Beth.

'No, just the adults. You won't miss much. These things are awfully boring.'

'Karen, where's the Savlon? I've burnt my hand.'

'In the drawer, where it's lived for the last twenty years,' she shouted at her husband. 'Run it under the cold tap first.' She turned to Beth and smiled a motherly smile. 'You'd think he just moved in.'

'You're hiding something,' said Beth. She wanted to press further, but more than that, she wanted a bacon roll to soothe her foul-tempered stomach.

'Nonsense, love,' her mother said. 'Everything is normal.'

Beth gave her an askew glance. 'That's a strange thing to say,' she chided. 'A very strange thing to say.'

Her mother's smiled never faltered. 'Ask your dad to set the video to record *X-Factor* tonight. Tell him we won't be in.'

'Why don't you? He can probably hear us.'

'I've got...things to do,' she said, and a faraway look came over her.

'You guys are weird,' said Beth, leaving her mother standing in the hall, the phone still in her hand. As she sat at the kitchen table, tucking into the badly burnt bacon roll — 'It's crispy, just how you like it' her dad said — she heard her mother rummaging through the crawlspace beneath the stairs. Ten minutes later, the sewing machine roared into life. It was a sound Beth hadn't heard for years. Her mother had been a keen seamstress once, and handmade most of Beth's dresses growing up. But the machine had been packed away when the mill closed, as both her parents took new jobs in Inverness, and time slipped effortlessly through their fingers.

'Mum said record *X-Factor,*' said Beth, as she sipped her coffee. She felt better now. She always did with some food in her belly.

'I will,' mumbled her father, engrossed in yesterday's paper. She excused herself from the table — there was only so much white-knuckle excitement she could handle — and made her way upstairs for a badly-needed shower. She passed the spare room, which had at one time been her father's office. The sewing machine whirred relentlessly from inside. Curious, Beth turned the handle. The door was locked. She knocked, but there was no response.

'Those guys are losing it,' she mumbled, and went back to bed.

6

THEY WERE, NATURALLY, THE ONLY PATRONS OF THE BOWLING alley. It was four o'clock, and the sun was still in the sky, hanging around like the last guest at a party. They sat together at their usual table between the broken pinball machine and the pool table that had been missing the cue ball for two years.

Beth had been the last to arrive, declining Grady's offer of a lift from his dad, blaming the unseasonal late-afternoon weather. She looked over at him and caught his eye. He smiled at her, and she smiled back, and when he put his hand on her thigh beneath the table, she let him.

Make your mind up, Beth.

'Hey guys, I've got an idea,' said Steve, thumping his fist off the table. Only Grady looked at him expectantly. Beth and Alice didn't bother, because they knew Steve made the same joke every Saturday night. Grady did too, but Beth supposed the eternal optimist living inside him still had a few years before life finally ground him into the dirt.

Steve nodded slowly, as if formulating a plan. He stood

and wandered around the table, holding his chin, then stopped. 'Let's get drunk,' he said, 'and bowl.'

'Can't argue with the man,' said Alice.

Beth rolled her eyes. 'Easy for you to say. You've missed several months of this.'

'He's like Peter Pan,' smiled Alice. 'He never grows up.'

'And,' said Steve, 'I look good in tights.'

'I pray I never have to see that,' said Beth.

Steve's eyes lit up. 'Wait here,' he said, hurrying from the table.

Beth looked at Alice. 'As if we have anywhere else to go.'

Alice gave her a side-eye. 'If he's putting on a pair of tights, I'm going home.'

An introductory drumbeat thundered from the jukebox, and an electric guitar kicked in with that uniquely eighties sound. It was *I Love Rock and Roll* by Joan Jett & The Black-hearts. Steve head-banged his way towards them, playing an appalling approximation of air guitar.

'Don't do it,' shouted Beth over the noise.

'Don't do what?' said Steve.

'Don't sing "I love to get drunk and bowl" over the chorus.'

Steve pulled a face. 'I'm not going to.'

'I don't believe you,' said Grady.

'I won't.'

Grady turned to Beth. 'He's going to do it.'

'I'm not!'

'Prove them wrong!' shouted Alice.

The chorus kicked in, and Steve swaggered up to Beth, stomping his feet and strumming his imaginary axe. '*I love to get drunk and bowl,*' he sang, crudely shoehorning in the extra syllable in his grotesquely off-key voice, '*so put fifty pence in the jukebox, Beth-y.*'

She smiled despite herself, as Steve continued to caper in front of her, thrusting his invisible guitar skyward. She playfully shoved him, but he kept singing, only stopping when she started to laugh.

'I did it!' he cried. 'I made Beth smile!'

'Fuck you,' she laughed, pushing away from the table, the legs of the chair screeching across the floor. 'I'm getting a beer.'

Steve pumped his fist. 'Yes! First round's on Beth.'

'Only if you stop singing,' she called back.

As she strolled to the bar, she felt a hand on her shoulder and she whirled round, letting out a yelp.

'Woah,' said Grady. 'Just wondered if you needed help carrying the drinks. Didn't mean to, y'know, make you shit yourself.'

'Sorry, I just...got a wee fright.'

His brow furrowed. 'You feeling okay?'

'Guess so. Didn't have a good sleep last night.'

Grady nodded. 'Because of me? I'm sorry if—'

'Not because of you.' She hesitated, unsure of how to word her thoughts. 'Last night, when I left, did you...*follow* me?'

His concern gave way to confusion. 'What do you mean?'

'I mean, did you follow me down the road for a while?'

He looked intently at her, probably wondering whether she was angling for a fight or not. 'No. I went straight in. I thought the conversation was over. Should I have followed you? I can never tell whether I'm supposed to follow you or leave you alone.'

'It's not about that.' She looked away, feeling ridiculous. 'Someone followed me. They touched me, but when I...ah, forget it.'

'Who did? Did Steve touch you?'

'Quiet,' she hissed, but Steve had heard anyway.

'You guys talking about me?'

They ignored him, and he went back to showing off in front of Alice.

'It wasn't Steve. It wasn't anyone. That's the thing...' She looked Grady in the eyes. 'Promise not to laugh.'

'I promise.'

She took a deep breath. 'When I looked round, there was no one there. But I swear, someone followed me.' She turned away, a hint of red creeping into her cheeks. 'I know, it sounds like a lot of bollocks.'

Grady took her hands in his. 'No. No, it doesn't.'

She stared at his earnest face. 'You've felt it too, haven't you?'

Grady didn't answer. He swallowed, working up the courage.

'I thought I—'

'You cunts wantin' a drink or not?' said Jack, leaning on the bar like it was keeping him vertical. 'I'm not gonna stand here all night while you two gaze into each other's eyes like a right pair of fannies.'

'Uh, yeah,' said Grady. He let Beth's hands slip from his grasp and headed for the bar. He turned to her. 'I'll get this round, okay?'

'What were you gonna say?' she insisted.

'We'll talk later. Take a seat, I'll bring the drinks over.'

And like that, the moment was gone.

She made her way back to the others. Steve was inputting everyone's names into the system. He went by his usual moniker, Spider, which he apparently believed made him sound cool. Currently though, he was arguing with Alice, holding her back with one beefy arm as she tried to delete the name he had given her.

'Don't you dare, Steve,' she said. 'Don't you fucking *dare* call me MILF.'

Steve bellowed with laughter and hit the big red button. 'Too late now!'

The word MILF flashed up on the ancient monitor in a font that made it look like an old sci-fi show.

'Steve!' shouted Alice.

'To be fair, you are a MILF,' said Beth.

'Don't encourage him,' said Alice, trying not to crack up.

Beth took her place by Alice's side and looked up at the scoreboard monitor to see her own name.

'Smiles,' she said to Steve. 'You put me down as Smiles.'

'Seemed appropriate,' Steve deadpanned.

She flashed a mirthless grin at him and turned to Alice. 'Kinda surprised to see you out two nights in a row.'

'Yeah, just for a little while. Gotta be back about six to let my mum go to that stupid meeting tonight.'

'God, my mum was acting so crazy about that. I think she was making a dress to wear to it.'

Alice giggled. 'Really?'

'Yeah, she got a call this morning, then ran and dug the sewing machine out from under the stairs. She was still locked in the spare room when I left.'

Alice shook her head. 'Parents are crazy.'

'At least you've got an excuse now,' said Steve, throwing a bowling ball in the air and catching it. Between his feet was a deep indentation in the wood, caused by this particular activity going drunkenly wrong a few years back. Jack had never noticed, and despite there being five lanes to use, Steve always insisted on this one.

'My mum was the same,' said Alice, ignoring Steve. 'She looked worried though. Her hands were shaking so much she almost dropped Eric. Said she was fine, but I don't believe her.'

'Jeez, maybe something's really up?'

'In Auchenmullan?' said Steve. 'It'll be fuckin' Inspector Larry telling us that the shoe tree is going to be made the official town monument, and we all have to dance naked round it every summer to ward off evil spirits.'

'All hail the shoe tree,' said Beth in her most ethereal voice, and Alice giggled again.

'You laugh now,' said Steve, lining up his first shot of the night, 'but you won't be laughing when you're skipping bare-arsed round that tree in front of Clive Moonie.'

'Oh god, not Clive,' shuddered Beth, and Steve jogged forwards and hurled the ball down the lane. It rolled along the wood with a comforting, familiar sound, slightly off-centre but curving towards the middle.

'Fucking strike!' he roared as all ten pins skittered across the smooth wooden lane. He turned to his friends, ready to do that stupid dance he did whenever he got a strike, then stopped.

'Steve...?' said Alice.

He stared at something behind them. Beth followed his gaze, past the bar, past Grady trying and failing to make small-talk with Jack, and towards the door.

It was open.

In the doorway, silhouetted against the glare of the setting sun, stood a solitary figure.

7

'WHO DO I HAVE TO *FUCK* TO GET A BEER IN THIS PLACE?' SAID a young voice.

An American voice.

A *female* voice.

Beth looked to Grady, but his eyes were locked on the interloper. Even Jack had stopped what he was doing, the beer from the tap pouring over the sides of the glass. Nothing fazed Jack, but it wasn't everyday someone new arrived in town. Beth couldn't remember the last time it had happened.

The girl entered, the door slamming behind her. She strode past Jack and Grady without a second glance, heading straight for the others. Her red hair danced over her shoulders, and she wore a puffy green jacket, a hiking rucksack slung over one lean shoulder. She dropped the bag at her feet and waited.

The face-off lasted an uncomfortably long time, no one sure what to do, no one sure what to say. Was she a mirage?

'Hi there,' said Grady, abandoning the bar and breaking the silence. He wandered over to the new girl and smiled.

'Excuse the slack-jawed looks on the faces of my friends, but we don't get many visitors round here.' He took her hand, and for a second, Beth thought he was going to kiss it.

'Grady, by the way,' he said as he shook her hand.

She smiled. 'Pleased to meet you, Grady By-the-way. I was beginning to think this place was deserted. Where is everyone?'

'Getting ready for the town meeting tonight,' said Beth.

The new girl just looked at her, as if a town meeting was a hopelessly alien concept.

'And what,' she said, 'the *whole* town is there?'

'That's right.'

'Like, *everybody*?'

'All the adults, yeah. There aren't too many of us left anymore.'

The girl nodded warily. 'Great. So I've arrived in Twin Peaks.'

'Pretty much,' said Beth. She realised she sounded apologetic. 'Anyway, I'm Beth. And you are...?'

'Thirsty. But you can call me Courtney.'

Grady signalled over to Jack. 'Hey Jack! A beer for Courtney.'

'Fuck off,' came the distant reply.

'Ah, that classic Scottish hospitality,' said Courtney.

Grady grinned. 'Don't worry, I'll get it myself.' He jogged away to retrieve a beer.

How gallant of him, thought Beth, with a trace of irritation.

Courtney turned her attention to Alice and Steve.

'What about you guys? Are you mute?'

Alice was about to answer, but Steve spoke over her, sucking in his gut and running a hand through his tousled hair.

'I'm Steve. Always nice to see a new face.' He paused for effect. 'Especially such a pretty one.'

Courtney shook her head. 'Corny, but I'll take it.'

'Can I speak now?' said Alice, 'or are you still flirting?'

Steve coloured, and grumbled, 'Be my guest.'

'My name's Alice, and I have one question, if you don't mind.'

'Shoot.'

'What the *fuck* are you doing in Auchenmullan?'

Courtney laughed. Grady trotted back, putting his hand on her arm, holding it there a little too long. She took the beer from him.

'Hitchhiking,' said Courtney. 'Land's End to John O'Groats, via the longest route possible. Some asshole in a BMW was gonna take me further, but he expected more in return than I was willing to give. When he stuck his hand up my shirt, I punched him in the throat and got out of there. Walked the last three miles into this deadbeat town — no offence — and here I am.'

'God,' said Beth, 'are you okay? Do you want to talk to the police?'

'Fuck no. I'm used to it. I can handle myself.' She pulled a flick-knife from her pocket, revealing the blade with the press of a button.

'Pay attention, Steve,' said Grady. 'She's armed.'

Steve punched him on the forearm, and Grady flinched in pain. Courtney laughed and unzipped her bulky jacket. Steve turned his attention back to her, his eyes dropping to her chest. 'So, where you gonna stay?'

'Are you asking me or my tits?'

'Uh,' replied Steve dumbly.

'She's not staying with you,' laughed Alice.

'Shut up, Al.'

Courtney shrugged. 'Where's good to crash for the night? I don't have much money.'

'Well,' said Grady, 'the Pine Lodge is nice. Only problem is, it closed down three years ago. That leaves...nowhere.'

'You could bed down in one of the many delightful abandoned houses,' said Beth. 'There're a couple hundred. Take your pick.'

'Shit,' said Courtney. 'Trust me to end up in the town that time forgot.' She slugged down some of her beer. 'So are you guys...it? Four of you?'

'That's right,' said Steve. 'Unless you count Jack, who's just a big kid at heart. Isn't that right, Jack?'

'Fuck off.'

Courtney chuckled. 'Is that all he can say?'

'That, and nothing else,' said Grady. If he was vying with Steve for Courtney's attention, Beth thought they were currently neck and neck. 'Rumour has it he was dropped on his head as a baby, and now all he can say is *fuck off*.'

Courtney laughed again, an infectious laugh, the kind accompanied by a flick of the hair and a flash of pearly white teeth. 'So what's the deal with this town meeting?'

'Dunno,' said Beth, getting in before Grady could crack one of his lame jokes. 'I think we're the only people not invited.'

'What about him?' said Courtney, jabbing a thumb in Jack's direction.

'You wanna ask him?' said Grady.

'I can guess the answer. So what do you think they do?' said Courtney with a gleam in her eye. 'Have a big orgy?'

'That's our parents you're talking about,' said Beth.

'Hey, parents need lovin' too,' said Courtney.

'Amen to that,' said Alice.

'Oh, you a mom?'

'Aye. Have a wee two-month-old. He—'

But Courtney had lost interest. She turned to Steve and Grady. 'And who's the father?'

'Oh god, neither of them,' said Alice. 'No offence, Grady.'

'What about me?' said Steve.

'You *should* be offended.'

Courtney turned back to Alice. 'So where is he? Skipped town? Dead?'

'Right the first time,' said Alice. She shared a look with Beth when Courtney went back to the boys, a look that said, *who the fuck does she think she is?*

'So what do you guys do round here for kicks?' said Courtney. 'Apart from bowling and attending secret town orgies.'

'We, uh...we get drunk,' said Steve. He looked to Grady. Grady looked to Beth.

Oh, so now *he needs help.*

'That's pretty much it,' she said.

Courtney nodded slowly. 'Wow. And I thought Wisconsin was lame.'

A tiny pang of annoyance needled at Beth. Sure, she hated Auchenmullan, and wished she could leave, but she didn't need some stuck-up American coming in and telling her what she already knew.

'It's not that bad here,' she said, surprising herself. Grady gave her a cockeyed glance. 'What? There's plenty of cool shit,' she continued, immediately regretting it.

'For example?' said Courtney.

'Yeah,' laughed Alice, 'like what?'

Flustered, Beth didn't know what to say. There was nothing to do here. Literally *nothing.* That's why they all met at Jack's, five, six, sometimes *seven* nights a week. Since The Vault had closed down, the nearest nightclub was in Inverness, although the neighbouring town of Kingussie had a karaoke night every Wednesday, arguably the only thing worse than nothing. Oh, and the shoe tree, of course, a tree with some trainers dangling from the branches that was the official meeting point from when they were kids. She fidgeted in her seat, wishing someone would step in and save her. Embarrassment burned her cheeks, and she hated Alice for joining in.

'We have a witch,' said Grady. He looked at Beth and smiled.

Thank you, she mouthed.

'A *witch*,' said Courtney. 'Seems unlikely, but I'm listening.'

'You ever hear the legend of Maggie Wall?' said Grady with a sly grin.

'No...should I?'

'Of course not,' said Steve. 'No one has.'

Grady's grin widened. He spoke with the theatrical inflections of a late night horror movie host. 'That's because the curse has been kept secret to protect the unwary.'

Steve coughed into his hand, but the cough was a barely disguised cry of 'Bollocks.'

Unfazed, Grady continued. 'You see, over three hundred years ago, Maggie Wall was sentenced to death for practicing witchcraft.'

'Uh-huh,' said Courtney, her eyebrows raised.

'That's right. She lived on the mountain, in a cottage near Cook's Point. Legend has it she was pregnant, and before they killed her, they—'

'Can't we leave this part out?' said Alice, subconsciously rubbing her belly.

'But it's the best part!' said Grady.

'What did they do?' asked Courtney, leaning in closer,

her hand on Grady's knee, which did *not* go unnoticed by Beth. Grady's smile broadened as he recounted the tale.

'They cut the baby out of her. Maggie was buried near her cottage, in a grave twenty feet deep, and a tree was planted over her so the roots would wrap around her corpse and keep her there.'

'And what about the baby?' said Courtney, her voice growing smaller.

'Well, the baby — or what was left of it after they sliced Maggie open and took it out — was put on trial. They sentenced it to—'

'That's enough,' said Alice. 'Please.'

Grady's smile faded. 'Sorry, Al. Anyway, they say that on a cloudless, moonlit night...*like tonight*...Maggie roams the mountain, searching for her missing baby.'

'Nobody says that,' said Steve dismissively.

'That's not true,' said Beth. 'My grandpa used to tell us that story, didn't he Al?'

Alice nodded. 'Gave me nightmares for weeks. My parents were raging.'

Courtney's eyes burned with a strange fire.

'I wanna go see the witch,' she said.

'You *did* hear the part about her being dead, aye?' said Alice.

'There's just a ruined cottage and her grave there now,' said Beth.

'The grave's still standing?' Courtney squeezed Grady's knee tighter. 'Oh my god, we should do a séance!'

'Jeez, what are we, thirteen years old?' said Beth. 'There's nothing up there but trees and thousands of midges.'

'Midges?'

'Little insects. Imagine a million tiny mosquitos nipping at your skin.'

'Midge season's past,' said Grady. He looked to Steve, the only one of them with a car. 'What do ya say, man? A visit to Maggie's Grave?'

Steve stifled a yawn. 'I dunno, it's a long drive.'

'And you've had a drink,' said Beth.

'So? There's no law against that.'

Beth gave up. There was no point in arguing with idiots. She walked over to get a beer and wondered if Grady would even notice she was gone.

Beth simmered by the bar, watching Grady and Steve compete for the attention — or affections — of Courtney.

'Better watch yourself,' said a voice, and Beth was surprised to find Jack behind the bar, his dishrag tucked into the side of his frayed jeans.

'What do you mean?'

Jack shrugged. 'Nothing. Boys like new things. Particularly small-town boys. They're like fuckin' magpies looking for shiny wee bracelets.'

'Not Grady,' said Beth, but they both suspected that wasn't true. He and Steve buzzed around Courtney like flies round shit, while she played with her hair and touched them on the arm and giggled.

'Aye, I'm sure you're right,' said Jack. He put another beer and a packet of salt-and-vinegar crisps in front of her.

'I'm outta money,' she said.

'This one's a freebie.'

Beth nodded. 'I can't blame him. Look at her...she's so pretty.'

Jack said nothing. Across the room Courtney threw back

her head and guffawed, her red hair like fire. 'I don't remember the last time I laughed,' she said to Jack.

'Want me to tell you a dirty joke?'

'I've heard them all, Jack. No, I mean *really* laughed. Or felt enthusiastic, or…happy.'

'You're better than this town,' said Jack quietly. 'You need to get out. All of you, before you end up like me.'

Beth smiled. 'But then who's gonna buy your beer?'

'I'll fuckin' drink it myself.'

They lapsed into a period of silence again.

'I don't know what I'm doing with my life,' said Beth.

'Neither do I,' said Jack. 'But you're young. You still have time to figure it out.'

'I hope so.' She looked at the grizzled barman, such a constant fixture in her life, at his sunken eyes and sagging chin and thinning hair. He looked as old as she felt. 'Thanks, Jack.'

His face reddened. 'Ach, fuck off,' he smiled. 'And by the way, your boyfriend is slow-dancing with that girl like it's fuckin' prom night.'

Beth looked round and saw Grady, both hands on Courtney's waist, shuffling to *Steppin' Out* by The Electric Light Orchestra. There was a sensation in her stomach she hadn't felt for a long time.

Jealousy?

Okay, so she and Grady were probably on the way out… but officially, they were still a couple. So why was he slow dancing with some girl, his hands snaking down to her hips?

Beth downed her beer, left the empty bottle on the counter and walked over to them. She tapped Grady on the shoulder.

'Oh hey, Beth,' he said casually.

'Let's go then,' she said.

Grady released Courtney and stepped back. 'Go where?'

Beth smiled. 'Let's pay a visit to Maggie Wall.'

'Alright!' shouted Steve, and that was all it took.

The decision had been made.

8

THEY GRABBED AS MANY BEERS AS THEY COULD CARRY AND lugged them to Steve's van. There was no fear of being pulled over by the police, not tonight. Inspector Carlisle, the only law for miles, would be chairing the town meeting. The streets were deserted, and as the alley was the last building on the edge of Auchenmullan, they wouldn't even have to drive past any homes. Only Jack would know where they were going, and Jack didn't give a shit.

The vehicle had once been used as part of Steve's dad's landscaping business, and still bore the Greener Pastures logo on the side, a grinning frog holding a pair of shears. When the business closed down, Steve inherited the van and attempted to turn it into a seventies-throwback shaggin' wagon, replete with mattresses and blankets and, in an unbearably tacky touch, a small mirrorball that swung from the roof. Unfortunately, he could never get rid of the smell of cut grass, and so the van smelled perpetually like garden waste, which Steve said was not conducive to lovemaking, though not quite in those words.

Alice took Beth aside as Grady and Steve piled the six-packs into the back of the van. 'You gonna be alright?' she asked quietly.

'I'll be fine,' said Beth, zipping up her parka. There was a chill in the air. 'Shame you can't come. We've not been up there for, god, how long?'

'A long time,' said Alice. 'Not since we were little kids. Just be careful, yeah?'

Beth smiled. She had a buzz from the beers, but something about Alice's demeanour set her on edge.

'Don't worry,' she said. 'Steve's only had a couple. He can drive us up there no problem.'

'It's not Steve, it's...'

'It's what?'

Alice sighed. 'It's nothing. Look, I'd better get going. Eric's probably hungry.'

'Beth, c'mon!' shouted Grady. 'We're ready!'

'Yeah, let's go raise the dead!' said Courtney with undisguised glee.

Beth gave Alice a look. 'I hate her.'

'She likes Grady,' said Alice.

'I've noticed. And she can keep her grubby little paws off him.'

Alice laughed softly. 'You tell her.'

'Well, I'd better head off. See you tomorrow?'

'Yeah. Why don't you come round, and we can hang out like old times? Watch a movie or something, let the boys do whatever boys do when we're not there.'

'So watch porn, then?'

'I think so.' Alice gently took Beth's hand. 'I mean it, Beth. Be careful up there.'

'You're weird, but okay, I will. Get home safe.'

'Beth!' roared Steve, his voice echoing through the valley.

'I'm coming! Jesus...'

She left Alice and jogged over to the van, pleased to see that Steve and Courtney were in the front, and Grady was alone in the back. She took a last look up at the sky, at the heavy clouds forming, and hoped it wouldn't snow while they were up the mountain.

Ah well, there was nothing she could do about the weather. She climbed into the van and sat beside Grady.

'Let's go see a witch,' said Steve, gunning the engine. The van lurched forward and stalled.

'Nice one,' said Grady.

'Not my fault. Engine's fucked.'

'Like everything else in this town,' said Courtney.

Steve tried again and this time they were off, the shimmering neon lights of Spring-heeled Jack's Bowling Alley fading into the distance. They took the main road out of town, the fields giving way to acres of pine forest that stretched into the twilight, the cloud-masked October sun descending behind the imposing mountain.

'See that?' said Steve, pointing out the window for Courtney's benefit. 'That's where she lived.'

'Right at the top?'

'Not quite. About three-quarters up.'

'Track only goes part of the way,' said Beth. 'We'll have to hike the rest.'

'In the dark?'

'Don't worry, babe,' said Steve. 'I'll hold your hand.'

'It's not my hand I'm worried about,' said Courtney.

Beth watched Auchenmullan from the back window, the lights of the town hall sparkling through grime-encrusted glass. They took the turnoff from the main road onto a dirt track, the wheels kicking up loose gravel that rattled against the underside of the van, and then they were climbing.

Up front, Steve finished a beer, crumpled the can, and tossed it out the window. The woods here were thick and wild, the park authorities no longer around to maintain them. They passed a sign reading 'Lookout Point,' which was riddled with holes from an air rifle belonging to Patrick Farquhar. Patrick had been two years older than Beth, the son of a farmer, and she had fancied the pants off him. She remembered the time he brought the air rifle to school in Kingussie and shot Mr Mulligan's tyres out from the Chemistry class window. She smiled at the thought.

So many memories.

Okay, so maybe Auchenmullan wasn't *all* bad. She had grown up here, and every person, every building, hell, every *tree* had some nostalgic memory wrapped around it. Shit, was she nearing the stage of drunken melancholy already? It was too early for that. She snaked an arm around Grady as the van, which was not built with country roads in mind, gasped its way up the incline, the elderly exhaust pipe wheezing.

'You ever think about leaving?' she said. 'Getting out of here, heading for the city?'

'You mean Inverness?'

'There are *other* cities, Grady. Glasgow. Edinburgh. London. Hell, what about Paris, or Milan, or Tokyo? Don't you want to see the world?'

'Yeah, but there are parts of Auchenmullan I've not seen. You know, I've never actually hiked to the top of the mountain. I might do that next year.'

Next year, Jesus Christ. He's so small-town.

They sat in silence for the rest of the trip, which was fine because Courtney and Steve spoke enough for all of them, Courtney deflecting Steve's dead-eyed attempts at flirting with practised ease, and yet somehow she ended up sitting between his legs as he 'taught' her how to drive.

Auchenmullan slipped from sight, and all Beth could see through the window was the darkness, and her own faded reflection staring back at her.

9

ALICE GAZED UP AT THE MOUNTAIN.

Occasionally she could make out the lights of the van as it wound its way up the tortuous dirt track, glancing between the trees until the woods became too thick for light to escape.

She was glad she wasn't with them. There was nothing to see up there. All that way, just to look at the crumbling ruin of an old lady's cottage.

Maggie Wall, The Witch of Auchenmullan.

She shook her head. People were so naïve back then. She had read once that magic mushrooms were to blame for so-called instances of witchcraft, people hallucinating and blaming — who else? — the women. Some things never change.

She wondered if the grave was still intact. Why not? There was no one left to vandalise it. It was funny how well she remembered it, as if she had been up there only last week. She could even smell the faint, fetid odour of damp pine needles mixed with rotten earth. God, it stank up there.

And the few times she *had* been up, she always felt like she was being watched.

Kind of like how she felt right now.

She passed Ken Thomson in his front garden and nodded at him. He waved cheerlessly back and went inside, the porch door slamming abruptly.

'Friendly,' she muttered.

Maybe Beth's right, she thought. *This is no place to bring up a child.*

Who was Eric going to play with? How would she get him to nursery, to school?

But what else could she do? She had no savings, no job. She couldn't afford the deposit for a rented flat, never mind buying one. And anyway, there was the matter of her mother. How could she leave her poor mum alone, especially as having a baby in the house had seemed to revitalise her? Alice had been worried about her mother for the last few years, ever since her father had died.

She still missed him every day, probably would forever. Whenever she got a new phone, she always ensured his mobile number was transferred over. It was silly, she knew. It's not like he was going to call anytime soon. And yet, she couldn't bring herself to delete it.

Delete.

Such a final, absolute word. She hated it.

So many absent fathers, she thought, trying to change the subject by thinking about Kevin, Eric's missing-in-action father. Where was he now? His family had hightailed it out of town within days of her telling Kevin about the pregnancy. They had just packed up and left without so much as a note.

Anything to avoid paying child support, that's what Steve had said.

They had spoken to Carlisle about it, and he promised her the police were looking out for the family, but so far, there had been no word. Sometimes, she wondered if Carlisle was telling the truth.

Speak of the devil.

There was his car, parked half-on the pavement at an angle, as if he had pulled over in a hurry. Alice's heart skipped a beat.

It was parked outside her house.

She jogged towards it. Was she wrong? Alice and her mother were one of the few families in town who still shared their street with neighbours — Pat and Bob Graham, a sweet old couple who lived two houses down. Was Carlisle's vehicle closer to them? She ran now, the wind picking up, impeding her progress. The police car was definitely outside her house.

A sick feeling wormed its way into her stomach.

Eric.

She was horrified to find herself hoping that something had happened to her mother.

Just not Eric. Please.

The thought appalled her, and yet it was undeniable. She loved her mum dearly, and would do anything for her, but if it came down to it, if she had to choose between them...

The front door was wide open. Alice's vision blurred, and she wiped tears from her eyes. She could hardly breathe, a combination of stark terror and her first real bit of cardio since giving birth. She burst into the hallway.

'Mum? Where are you? Is Eric okay?'

There was no answer. The living room was empty, the TV on, some nature show playing on the screen. A steaming cup of freshly made coffee smouldered on the table, a half-eaten bowl of pasta next to it.

That was when she noticed the blood.

It stained the sofa. Not a lot, but enough to raise her stress levels to near-meltdown.

'Mum!' she screamed. She turned to leave the room, to run up the stairs, and there he was, right behind her.

A man, blocking her route.

She threw herself at him, balling her fists and pounding against his chest.

'Where's my baby?'

'Alice, calm down, please,' said Inspector Carlisle as he gripped her forearms and held her tight.

'Where's Eric?' sobbed Alice. 'What happened? Where are they?' She was babbling, her eyes darting back and forth as she struggled to break free.

'Your son is fine, don't worry about him,' said Carlisle in a calm, even voice. It did nothing to reassure her.

'I need to see him, I need—'

He struck her across the face with an open hand. The sound was a whip-crack in the still air of the room, and she stared at him in shock, her cheek stinging. She hadn't been slapped since, what, primary school?

'You need to calm down,' said Carlisle, enunciating every syllable. He let go of her, and Alice put a hand to her face, shrinking back. On the telly behind her, someone was droning on about the lifespan of giant redwood trees.

'What happened?' she asked in a small voice.

'It's your mother,' he said. 'Alice...I'm afraid she's dead.'

She got that feeling in her stomach like when a car goes over a bump, but it wasn't fleeting. It kept going, over and over, her guts churning. She moved to sit and remembered the bloodstains on the sofa, but by then it was too late and she could no longer stand on legs that trembled with shredded nerves. Instead she fell forwards into the waiting arms of Carlisle. He held her, his big arms enveloping her, and she cried against his jacket.

'Where's Eric?' she managed to say.

'He's at the station. I took him there and left him with Judy Guthrie. He's safe, don't worry.'

'And...my mum?'

'She's upstairs. I've called an ambulance, but it won't be here for another hour.'

'I want to see her.'

'That's not a good idea,' said Carlisle. He gently pushed her away from him, holding on to her shoulders. 'Listen, Alice. This will come as a shock to you, so why don't you sit down?'

'No,' she said, afraid that if she did, she would never get back up again. 'I need to see her. I have to. What happened?'

Carlisle grimaced. He walked over to the TV and nudged the off switch. The room fell silent apart from the infuriating tick of the wall clock. Alice rarely noticed it, as whenever she was in the living room, her mother was there too, and the TV was invariably on.

Never again.

Fresh tears dribbled down her cheeks.

'Tell me,' she whispered.

Carlisle took a troubled breath and looked her in the eyes. 'Alice...your mother killed herself.'

'No,' she said, backing up against the sofa, falling onto it. 'No, you're wrong.'

'Pat Graham reported a gunshot. I came to investigate and found her upstairs.'

Alice tried to process the information, but a flashing ERROR sign was all she could visualise. 'She wouldn't. Why would…it's not possible. We don't…we don't have a gun. It's Scotland, no one has guns…'

'I'm sorry, Alice. Come on, I'll drive you to the station, and you can see the wee one. You'd like that, wouldn't you?'

'I want to see the body,' she said. 'I have to know it's her.'

'I told you, it's not a good idea. The shot was…' He swallowed, the sound filling the room, and started again. 'The shot was to the face. You wouldn't recognise her.' Then, he added, 'There's nothing left.'

Alice leaned back against the sofa. She felt too hot in her big winter jacket, the central heating cranked to the max the way her mother liked it. She stared at the family portraits on the wall opposite, hanging above the black void of the TV screen.

There was her parents' wedding photo, and several holiday snaps — one taken in Greece (she was so young she no longer remembered it), one on the banks of Loch Ness (she had thought she'd seen Nessie but it was just a tree uprooted by a storm), and one in this very room, shot by a professional photographer from Inverness for her sixteenth birthday.

Then there was the latest addition.

A photo of Eric.

He was in Alice's arms, shortly after the birth. She hated herself in the photo, her face red and puffy and tired, hair plastered to her brow with sweat. In the background was her mother, beaming with pride, her eyes brimming with adoration for her beloved grandchild.

There was no way she would kill herself.

It wasn't just *unlikely*, or *out-of-character*. It was impossible. Oh, she knew you could never really know what was going on beneath the surface, what dark thoughts tortured a person's mind at night, but she also knew her mother would *never* leave her and Eric alone.

Alice got unsteadily to her feet.

'Sit a moment,' said Carlisle. 'When you feel up to it, we'll get in my car and drive to the station.'

'Show me the body,' she said. Carlisle seemed taken aback by the conviction in her voice.

'No. I've already made a positive identification.' He walked to the window and peered through the floral curtains. Night had fallen quickly across the valley.

'Why are there bloodstains on the sofa?' said Alice.

He turned sharply. 'What did you say?'

'The blood...' she said, pointing towards the dark red spots on the sofa, but already she knew. She could see it in his expression, clear as day. He started to speak, changed his mind, stuttered something.

It was all Alice needed to know.

She ran for the door, Carlisle giving chase. He stretched out a hand and grabbed the hood of her jacket, but she slipped free of the garment and made it into the hall, racing up the stairs.

'Stop!' shouted Carlisle. He was out of shape. Five years of sitting at a desk will do that to even the finest cop, and Carlisle was far from the best the police force had to offer.

Alice heard his boots clump onto the stairs, but she was already at the top. On the hall landing she had a choice to make. There were four doors; her mother's bedroom, her own bedroom, the bathroom, and the spare room. A sliver of light spilled out beneath the door to her mother's room, and she chose that one, knowing she would only have time to check one room before Carlisle caught up to her. She slammed into the door shoulder-first. It swung open on creaking hinges, slamming into the wardrobe with a colossal bang.

'Oh god,' she cried.

A body lay on the bed, covered by a thin white sheet. She looked at the head, where the fabric was wet and crimson and stuck to the shattered face. But there was another, larger blood patch, lower down. It didn't make sense. She heard Carlisle nearing the top of the stairs, his footsteps growing louder, and she whipped the sheet off the body. Her mother lay there in her pyjamas and dressing gown, barely recognisable, her face a collapsed mass of blood and tissue.

But she had also been shot in the stomach.

She didn't kill herself, her mind screamed at her. *She was murdered.*

'No,' whimpered Alice. She whirled as Carlisle entered the room, his face deformed with fury.

'You killed her,' she said, as he pulled the police baton from his belt and raised it high. 'You killed my mum.'

'I had to,' said Carlisle, and then he brought the baton crashing down across her skull and everything went dark.

10

'HERE WE ARE,' ANNOUNCED STEVE, AS THE VAN SHUDDERED to a halt.

In front of them the track ended in a mound of dirt, as if whoever had constructed it had given up in despair. A wall of ancient trees towered menacingly over them, the van's powerful headlights dwarfed into insignificance.

Steve turned to Grady.

'Grab the beers, man,' he said.

'I can't carry them all,' huffed Grady. They were the first words he had spoken in a long time, and his voice sounded gravelly.

Beth cranked open the back doors and stepped out, the refreshing night breeze hitting her hard, carrying with it the smell of pine. It brought her back to her childhood. Sure, she could smell it in town, but not like this. God, it was overpowering. Memories flooded her subconscious, of trips through the woods with her family, of summers spent playing in the forest with her friends. She listened a moment to the sound of water dripping from the branches. One droplet landed on her forehead and she closed her eyes, breathing in the mountain air and listening to Courtney's piercing voice from inside the van.

'There's nothing but a bunch of fucking trees,' she said.

Beth almost smiled.

To you, maybe.

But to Beth, this was a photo album, a journal. Her life story.

So why are you so keen to get away?

Not interested in an argument with herself, she turned to watch Grady struggling with three six-packs.

'A little help here?' he called to Steve, as he blundered towards the driver's door.

It opened and Courtney climbed out over Steve. He put his hands on her waist to assist her, and she landed in the tall grass. Steve fixed the crotch of his jeans and followed her out.

'God, it's not changed,' said Beth. It was as if she had never been away. She felt like a child again, half-expecting her grandpa to emerge from the trees with his rucksack and tent and lopsided grin.

'Where's the bathroom?' said Courtney, and Beth snorted.

'Just next to the gift shop,' she muttered. Only Grady heard, and he chuckled.

It was cold out, and Beth shivered in her fleece-lined jacket. She looked down at her running shoes — which was a laugh, because she had never actually gone running in them — and hoped the forest trail wouldn't be too muddy. The tyres of the van were already sinking into the soft ground.

'What if the van gets stuck?' she said.

Steve reluctantly let go of Courtney and looked at the wheels. He nodded thoughtfully.

'You're right,' he said. 'Give me a minute.'

He climbed back into the van while Courtney angrily shoved her hands in her pockets. It reminded Beth of Alice as a kid, pouting and whining when she didn't get her way, and she suddenly wished Alice was here with them now.

Steve performed a tight three-point turn, bumping one of the brake lights against a tree and cracking it. In his mildly drunken state, he didn't seem to notice.

'Hey, Courtney,' said Grady, tottering back and forth with the beers balanced precariously on outstretched arms. 'Mind taking one of the six packs?'

She scrunched up her face. 'Ugh, *no.*'

The van now facing downhill, Steve reversed it up a small embankment where the ground was thick with ferns and grass. 'How's that?' he shouted out the window.

'Better,' said Beth. 'Now go help Grady before his arms fall off.' Grady shot her a look, but she shrugged, and said, 'Well, they *might.*'

Steve exited the van with a halogen torch in his hand. He shone it into Beth's face to annoy her, then held it under his chin and stalked towards Courtney.

'Are you ready...*to meet Maggie Wall?*'

'Anytime today would be great,' she said. 'I'm freezing my ass off out here. Why's this country so cold all the time?'

'Come on, I'll keep you warm,' he cooed, putting his arm around her. She clung to him like a limpet and they took off into the dense woods, leaving Grady and Beth by the van.

'Think they've forgotten about us,' said Grady.

'You surprised? Steve's practically humping her leg.'

Beth walked to the unlocked van and opened the back doors. 'We don't need all these beers. We'll take one pack and leave the rest here for when we come back.'

'Good idea,' said Grady.

They dumped the booze, closed the doors, and followed the light of Steve's torch. Already, it was surprisingly far ahead, swooning past trees as the serpentine path wound its way through the forest. In the still of the night, they could hear Courtney bombarding Steve with questions.

'How do you know where we're going?' she asked.

He shone the beam at their feet. 'See those wee stones? They're markers. Take you right to Maggie's cottage.'

'Did you put them down?'

'No, they were here long before I was born.'

'So who did?'

'I don't know.'

'I'm hungry, you bring any snacks?'

Grady smiled and nudged Beth with his elbow. 'You regretting this yet?'

'Ever since we left.' She winced. 'Not because of you...I mean us...'

'It's okay, let's try to enjoy ourselves. Let's...'

He didn't seem to know how to finish, which Beth supposed summed up their relationship pretty succinctly. When had they stopped communicating? She wanted to tell him she was sorry, and that it was all her fault, even though it wasn't, not entirely, but Grady was right. They could discuss it tomorrow. There was always tomorrow.

'I never should've mentioned Maggie Wall,' said Grady.

'It was my fault,' said Beth. 'I told her there were fun things to do here.'

'I did wonder if you'd been replaced by a pod person.'

'I looked like an idiot.'

Grady laughed. 'What were you going to say if I hadn't stepped in?'

'Easy. I would have said...'

'I'm waiting.'

Beth giggled. 'Let me finish. There's...the shoe tree.'

'The shoe tree.'

'That's right.'

'You think she's come all the way from America to see a pair of shoes hanging from a tree?'

'It's a local landmark.'

Grady adopted a tone of mock indignance. 'Fine, I'll give you the shoe tree. What else?'

Beth thought for a moment. 'St Mary's Hump,' she said proudly.

'Okay, now you're just making shit up.'

'No, no,' she laughed, 'it's the mound of grass near the old garage. There used to be standing stones there, until someone stole them.'

'God, maybe you're right. This town *is* sad,' said Grady.

She had nothing to say to that.

The path grew fainter, the lichen-coated markers hidden behind overgrown bushes or missing altogether. The trees closed in on them, obscuring the moonlight, but although Steve and Courtney were far ahead of them and out of sight, it didn't seem to matter. They followed the path without thinking, as if an invisible entity was leading them by the hand.

'We're here,' said Grady. Beth looked at him, puzzled, then followed his gaze. Before her, on the edge of a clearing, stood Steve and Courtney, and beyond them, Maggie's cottage.

They had arrived.

'That was quicker than I remembered,' said Beth.

'You were younger last time you came here,' said Grady. 'Shorter legs.'

She gave him a sideways glance. 'I wasn't a *penguin*.'

Courtney turned to them. 'You guys have penguins up here?'

'What?' said Beth. 'No, of course—'

'It's cold enough for penguins,' interrupted Courtney. Beth bit back an interruption of her own, and Courtney turned to Steve. 'Looks like no one's been up here for years.'

'Well, why would anyone want to?' said Steve, his hand tucked snugly into the waistband of her jeans.

'I dunno,' she said. 'To make out or something?'

'Hell of a trek just to get your end away,' said Steve, oblivious to the irony of why he was here.

'And I thought romance was dead,' said Beth.

Steve turned to her. 'Aye, says you that once got caught shagging in the toilets at Jack's.'

'Twice,' corrected Beth. 'The presidential suite at the Hilton was all booked out.'

'Come on,' said Courtney, 'I'm getting bored.'

Beth thought she heard Steve sigh. Even *he* sounded fed up with Courtney's incessant moaning. He led the way, the torchlight picking out branches and strange, small creatures that skittered through the undergrowth.

Beth followed, holding one hand up in front of her to catch any spiderwebs before they broke across her face, until they were fully out of the woods and standing in the clearing, the trees encircling them. In the cool blue of the moonlight, she could make out the shape of Maggie Wall's cottage. She was surprised to see it still stood.

'They don't make 'em like they used to,' she said for no one's benefit but her own.

'Is this it?' sneered Courtney. 'You brought me all the way up here to see an old cabin? My *uncle* lives in a place like this, and he's creepier than any witch.'

'No,' said Steve, trying to inject some enthusiasm into

proceedings. 'This is just where she *lived*. Her grave is round back. That's the really awesome part.'

'I'm cold,' shivered Courtney. She pouted at Steve. 'Build me a fire.'

Yes, your majesty, thought Beth.

Instead, she said, 'You guys go to the grave. We'll stay here and get a fire going.'

Grady gave her a despairing glance.

'Sounds good to me,' said Steve. He handed Beth the torch. 'Here, take this. I know the way.'

'Oooh, big man,' said Beth.

Steve gave her the finger.

'Jesus,' said Courtney. She rubbed her head against his shoulder, her movements catlike. 'You gonna warm me up or what?'

'Later guys,' smiled Steve.

'Yeah,' said Courtney. 'Hopefully *much* later.' She gave Steve an alluring look that turned Beth's stomach, and the two of them walked away, taking a wide berth around the cottage. Beth heard their footsteps, the soft crackle of autumn leaves crunching underfoot, but they were soon devoured by the night. Then, from out of nowhere, came Courtney's distant voice.

'Hurry up you idiot, I'm horny.'

'Young love,' said Beth, and Grady laughed out loud.

'Well, want a beer?' he said.

'Like you wouldn't believe.'

She switched off the torch and set the beers on the ground, letting the darkness envelop her. The stars were bright, the moon fat and white, and her thoughts turned once more to camping trips with her grandfather, which in turn led to thinking about Alice, and her own family, and Maggie Wall, and—

Wait. Maggie Wall? Jesus, would that bitch get out of her head for, like, five minutes?

She flicked the torch back on to grab a beer.

'Keep it off,' said Grady.

'I'm just—'

'I said switch the fucking torch off.'

She turned to him, pointing the beam at his face. 'What? Who the fuck do—'

'Beth, *please.*'

There was something about the way he spoke that defused her anger, something in his voice.

Fear?

She thought so, yes. In all their years together, Grady had never raised his voice at her.

'What is it?' she said, killing the torchlight.

'Where did Steve and Courtney go?'

Christ, was that it?

'Where were you thirty seconds ago? They've gone to see the grave, and by see the grave, I mean fuck each other silly.'

'Yeah, but did you *see* where they went?'

Beth laughed, but it was a strange, scared-sounding laugh. 'What's wrong with you? You're freaking me out.'

'Did you *see* them?'

'I saw them walk off, yeah.'

'So they didn't go into the cottage?'

'No, Grady,' she said, frightened sarcasm dripping from her words, *'They didn't go into the cottage.'*

'So *nobody* went into the cottage,' snapped Grady.

'Fuck's sake, are you mental? No! No one did, and stop saying *cottage*, it's losing all meaning.'

'Then who's in there?' he said.

A chill ran down Beth's spine.

'What do you mean?' she said in an odd, hollow voice.

Grady's breathing was slow and heavy. 'Someone's in there...*right...now.*'

Beth turned. At first she saw nothing but the swaying trees against the dark blue of the sky.

'What are you on about?' she said, anger bubbling to the surface once more. 'There's no one here but us.'

Then she saw it.

Her blood froze, and she said nothing, for there was nothing to say.

There, in the window of Maggie's cottage, flickered a single candle.

11

AT FIRST, ALICE THOUGHT SHE WAS AT SEA.

She couldn't figure out how or why this had happened, but her body rocked gently back and forth on undulating waves, and she went with the fantasy. It was a soothing sensation, and she wondered if this was how Eric felt when she rocked him in her arms.

Eric.

Her eyes snapped open. Where was she? A car? Her head throbbed in pain and frustration. She attempted to raise her hands, to touch the area that pulsed waves of agony throughout her cranium, and found her wrists were cuffed. It was dark outside. Night. She remembered her mother, lying in a pool of blood. A dream?

No. Not a dream. Not even a nightmare.

She looked at Carlisle in the driver's seat, his eyes fixed on the road, the dashboard lights turning his grim face a sickly yellow.

'You hit me,' she said softly.

He refused to meet her gaze.

'I didn't expect you home so early,' he said. 'That whole

mess should have been cleaned up before you arrived.' He spoke in a matter-of-fact voice, like someone in a call centre reading from a script.

Oh yes, I see, so your mother's dead? Have you tried switching her off and on again?

'Why did you do it?' she asked, forcing the words out. God, she needed paracetamol. Or better yet, some Tramadol. She knew her mum kept some on the top shelf of the bathroom cabinet for when her arthritis pain became too much. She thought of her, and the tears came.

Carlisle grunted, and she felt like a bothersome child asking too many questions. It angered her.

'I didn't want to kill her,' he said. 'She wouldn't...cooperate.'

'What do you *mean?*' said Alice. 'Why did you do it? Where's my baby? And where the *fuck* are we going?'

Carlisle said nothing, but she saw his hands grip the steering wheel tighter.

'Tell me!' she roared. 'Tell me, or else I swear to god, I'll...I'll...'

'You'll what? Call the police? Stupid girl, I *am* the police.'

I put the Law in Lawrence, that's what he always says.

The vehicle pulled sharply off the road and Alice had a crazed vision of him dragging her from the car and beating her to death in the bushes. Why not? He was insane, a maniac, a kidnapper, a *murderer*. Could she fight him off? No. She was weak and tired, and he was a burly bastard over six-feet-tall. He could do whatever he liked with her. The idea made her sick. What if he—

Neon light suddenly bathed the interior of the car, and Alice knew that unless they had taken a wrong turn and ended up in Tokyo, Carlisle had driven her to the police station. It was a desolate looking building, and — much like everything else in Auchenmullan — badly in need of a fresh coat of paint. The glowing blue tube lights had originally spelled POLICE, but several letters had been smashed over the years and never replaced. It now read P I E.

The pie station, that was what Beth called it. Alice couldn't recall the last time she had set foot inside.

'We're going to get out of the car,' said Carlisle, turning the key until the engine died. 'And I don't want you to make a sound.'

'Where's my baby? Where's Eric? Please, I'll do anything you say, just give me my baby.' She broke down, sobbing, unable to hide her head in her cuffed hands. Snot dribbled into her mouth, and at that moment, she felt useless, a failure. Her son was gone, and here she was, snivelling and begging the man who took Eric and killed her mum.

'He's inside,' said Carlisle. He finally turned to look at her, then reached into his pocket.

A gun, he's got a gun.

It was a tissue. He held it out to her.

'I can't,' said Alice, glancing at the handcuffs.

'Shit,' he said. He stuffed the tissue back into his pocket and rubbed his forehead like all this was too much for him. 'Listen...in a minute, I'm going to get out. I'll come round and open your door, unlock the handcuffs, and then we walk into the station together, okay?'

She nodded.

'Tell me you can do that,' he said. 'No nonsense. Your son is in there waiting for you. Do you want to see him?'

'I do,' she sniffed.

'So tell me you'll be a good girl.'

'I'll be good.'

'No nonsense?'

'No nonsense. I promise.'

'Alright. You're a nice lassie at heart. I *know* you are. But why did you have to...' he trailed off.

'What?'

'Doesn't matter. You ready?' He looked at her with sympathy in his eyes. So why was he doing this? Was someone making him? Was her mother actually a dangerous criminal, and Carlisle had saved her and Eric from catastrophe? So many questions, and no answers forthcoming.

He got out of the car and slammed the door behind him, trudging round to Alice's side.

It's okay, you're about to see Eric. You can hold him and kiss him and never let him go, never let him out of your sight again.

Would any of this have happened if she had stayed home tonight? Was it all her fault? She should never have gone to the alley, not two nights in a row. How selfish of her...how self-indulgent.

If you'd stayed home, you'd be dead too. At least this way Eric has a chance.

The door opened and Carlisle leaned in, an aged silver key in his hand. He gave her a quick look that said *don't even think about it* and unlocked the cuffs. She stretched her arms, then rubbed her head where he had struck her with the baton. The area was clotted with dried blood.

'Can you walk?' he said.

'I think so.'

She slowly lifted her legs out of the vehicle and planted her feet on the grass. Carlisle took her arm and helped her stand. Her skull felt swollen, and she imagined a cartoonish bump on the top of it, like the roadrunner had just dropped an Acme anvil on her head. She took a few deep breaths and glanced around to see if anyone was watching. Despite everything, a tiny part of her was still concerned with the humiliation of being led into the police station in handcuffs. It was ridiculous, she knew, but the idea helped ground her in a reality she understood.

'Come on,' said Carlisle. His grip was strong — as if she could run anywhere when her head felt like it was about to split open and disgorge its contents onto the lawn — and he started towards the station.

The pie station.

She had no choice but to follow. Eric was in there.

Wasn't he?

He's not in there, he's dead.

Panic once more twisted its knife in her gut. She recalled the dreams she had experienced the first month after giving birth, horrifying visions in which Eric was crawling up the curtains, too high for her to reach, or climbing into the oven or the fridge and the door accidentally closing behind him. The terror had been immense, and she frequently woke screaming, soaked in sweat.

Now those dreams were becoming reality.

She tried to squirm free of Carlisle's grasp.

'You promised,' he said, and Alice almost laughed at the absurdity. Instead, she yelled.

'Help! Someone help me, please!'

He lifted her roughly over his shoulder like he was rescuing her from a burning building. Alice struggled, pounding her fists on his back, but Carlisle was too strong. She saw figures across the road, Clare Hughes and her husband, who's name Alice could never remember.

'Help!' she screamed. *'He killed my mum! He's taken my baby!'*

The Hughes watched a moment, then turned their backs and quickly retreated.

'Where are you going? Help me! Help!'

Carlisle kicked open the door, and then they were inside, cut off from the rest of the world. The door closed heavily behind them, echoing throughout the empty reception. The station was deserted, no sign of dear old Judy Guthrie tending to Eric, no evidence that anyone had even *been* here in the last few weeks.

A dusty monitor sat atop an oak desk, the computer chair behind it facing the wall as if in a huff. There was an old-fashioned WANTED poster hanging from its last shred of Blu Tack, a black-and-white illustration of Carlisle scribbled on it. WANTED FOR CRIMES AGAINST FASHION, it said. LAWRENCE CARLISLE. REWARD FOR CAPTURE: THE AFTERNOON OFF.

'Please,' said Alice. 'Where are you taking me?'

Carlisle paid no attention, pushing his way through a set of swing doors. He carried on down a hallway, Alice still slung over his shoulder, and then they were in the jail block, which consisted of one sad little cell. Auchenmullan was hardly a hotbed of criminal activity, even back when people used to live here.

Still Alice struggled, growing wearier with each attempt to break free. It wasn't exactly a fair fight. Carlisle wandered into the cell and deposited her on the bed. When she tried to sit, he pushed her onto the mattress, the springs jabbing uncomfortably into her back through the wafer-thin foam. She kicked out, aiming for his crotch but catching him on his thigh, and he angrily pinned her to the bed by her shoulders, his face inches from hers.

'I don't want to hurt you,' he said, the smell of pepperoni and coffee on his breath. His palms pressed against her collarbone, nails digging into her flesh. 'But if I have to, I will.'

She gave him a couple of half-hearted slaps, but knew it

was over. She couldn't win, not right now. Carlisle released her and stood, backing out of the cell. The door closed behind him and he locked it. The *clunk* of the lock had a chilling finality to it.

You might never get out of here alive, she thought.

But she couldn't believe that. This was Auchenmullan.

This was her *home*.

'Please,' she said, as Carlisle stood on the other side of the bars, watching her like she was a zoo animal. 'Just tell me. Where's Eric?'

He scratched at his nose, cleared his throat. 'You have no reason to believe me, but I'm telling you God's honest truth. Your son is safe and well.'

'Can I see him?' she croaked.

'You will. Tonight.'

'Please, I need him. I need to know he's okay.'

'You have my word,' said Carlisle. 'For now, that's the best I can do.' He turned to leave, then paused. 'I really am sorry,' he said without looking at her.

'Why did you kill her?' said Alice. She wiped a tear from her cheek. 'Why did you kill my mum?'

He waited a long time, seemingly weighing up his options. Outside, Evelyn Ronald's dog howled. He was early tonight.

'Your mother knew what had to be done,' Carlisle said slowly. 'She knew the risks involved. We *all* did. This could have been avoided, but when the time came, she couldn't do it. She just couldn't bring herself to do it.'

'Do what?' said Alice. *'Do what, you bastard?'*

Carlisle sighed. 'She wouldn't give up the baby.'

12

'Is it much further?' asked Courtney.

Steve could tell she was getting bored. She had barely spoken to him since they left Grady and Beth, and kept yawning. He couldn't blame her. His chat had dried up. Man, he was out of practice! All he could think about was the way her right breast pressed into his side, and how his hand was tucked into the back of her jeans, into her underwear, his fingers pressing against the curve of her buttock. On top of all that, his growing erection made it difficult to walk like a normal person.

Steve hadn't had sex in almost a year, and the anticipation was playing havoc with his thoughts.

'Almost there,' he said. She didn't reply. He looked around, trying to think of something to say, something amusing, something...*debonair*. What he came out with was, 'You like trees?'

She gave him an annoyed glance.

'Yes,' she said. 'Trees get me *so wet.*'

Shit, he thought. *That was stupid.*

It was. For all his bravado and cocksure attitude, Steve

was nervous. He took one of the beers that jangled in his pocket and popped the cap with his teeth, hoping it would impress her. 'Here, this'll keep you warm.'

She took it and said nothing, which he hoped was her way of saying thanks. He didn't think he'd ever actually met a real-life American before, only seen them in films. God, how exotic! And now here they were, just him, her...and Maggie Wall.

'I used to come here as a kid,' he said, hoping to spark some conversation while she drank. 'We'd build a shelter out of twigs, roast marshmallows over the fire.'

She stopped, her lips glistening in the moonlight. 'You writing your memoirs?'

'What?'

'I don't need your life story. I just want to fuck you on some dumb witch's grave, okay?'

'Oh,' he said. She tilted her head back and downed the rest of the beer, some of it trickling down her chin, and Steve took the opportunity to adjust his dick. God, she was hot. Well, not literally. Her skin was cold. Soft, but cold. She tossed the bottle to the side, where it hit a tree, the glass shattering.

They resumed walking. Steve's fingers probed deeper into her jeans until he cupped one whole ass cheek. He squeezed it between his fingers, and she slapped his hand and glared at him.

'Not here,' she said, her tone as chilly as her flesh. 'At the grave.'

'No problem,' grinned Steve. He reached out with his free hand and pulled aside a large fern.

'Oh *shit*,' said Courtney. For the first time since they had arrived, she sounded genuinely interested. *Impressed*, even.

Maggie Wall's grave marker stood before them. The

lower half was a pyramid of rocks up to Steve's shoulder-height, the stones coated in moss and crispy fungus. It had been constructed around a tree that had long-since withered and died, the trunk carved into a crude cross that stood at least twelve-feet-high. The old tree had been warped by vines that wound their way protectively over the cross, its roots protruding between the pyramid's stones, seeming to bind the forbidding edifice together.

A piece of slate had been fastened to the pyramid, a faded inscription carved upon it. Courtney leaned in closer.

'What does it say?'

Steve fumbled a lighter from his pocket. He didn't smoke, he just thought carrying a lighter made him look sophisticated. He flicked the wheel and nothing happened. The second attempt offered an equally dismal result.

'First time?' said Courtney with a sneer.

His hand was trembling. He felt both annoyed and aroused, which was a curious combination. Reluctantly, he removed his other hand from Courtney's jeans, trailing his fingers along the smooth skin of her ass, and tried the lighter again, shielding it from the wind. This time a small flame appeared, illuminating the plaque, and Steve breathed a deep sigh of relief, which almost blew the flame out again.

MAGGIE WALL BURIED HERE AS A WITCH

1657

Courtney reached out and touched it, running her fingertips over the writing. Steve stepped closer and slipped his arm around her. In the light, she looked like one of those old paintings he remembered from school. He turned her to face him, and kissed her on the lips.

She squirmed out of his grasp.

'Oh, are you a kisser?'

'I...'

'It's fine,' she said, but he could practically hear her eyes rolling. Should he try again? He moved in, his hands finding her waist, kissing her harder. She responded by biting down on his lip.

'Ow.'

'It's too cold,' she purred, turning her back on him and crossing her arms. 'Build me a fire.'

He put his arms around her, nuzzling her neck, and she wriggled free.

'I'm serious.'

Steve tried not to lose what little cool he had left. 'Aw c'mon, that's too much work. Beth's building one at the cottage.'

'But I told you, I'm cold.'

'Yeah,' said Steve, thinking, *I heard you the first hundred times*. Part of him wanted to push her over, run back to the van, and leave her on the mountain. Let her find her own way home. He knew he would never do that, but the idea still made him smile.

Courtney stared at Maggie's grave. 'What about that?'

'What about what?'

'Set it on fire.'

'What?'

'The cross, dumbass. It's made of wood, isn't it?'

Most trees are, he thought, and laughed. Then he realised she was serious. 'We can't do that.'

She tilted her head at him. 'Haven't you ever wanted to fuck in front of a burning cross?'

Steve hadn't, but felt this wasn't the time to say so.

'It'll never catch fire,' he said. 'The wood's too wet.'

'At least something is.'

'Look, I...'

She turned to face him. In the shimmering orange glow of the lighter, she was the most beautiful thing Steve had ever seen. In fact, she didn't even look like the same person.

She unzipped her jacket, took his hand, and placed it on her breast, the thin cotton of her shirt all that stood between them.

No wonder she's cold, thought Steve. *She's not dressed for a Scottish winter.*

Then he remembered where he was and what he was doing, and chuckled at the stupidity of his thoughts.

'Set the cross on fire,' said Courtney, as her hands found his belt buckle and worked to unclasp it. 'Would you do that for me? Please?'

'You know she's buried right underneath us?' His dry mouth clicked as he spoke. She unsnapped two of the poppers on her shirt and moved his hand inside, to the soft roundness of her bare breast.

'I know,' she said. 'That's what makes it so hot.'

He could feel her heart beating, the vibrations coursing through his own body. He swallowed, and it was ludicrously loud.

'Okay, I'll try.'

He waited a moment, enjoying the touch of her skin, then moved the lighter closer to the cross, ready for it to fizzle out on contact. He hoped she would still have sex with him even if he couldn't get it to light. It had been so long! His cock throbbed in his pants and he knew he'd have to be careful if he wanted this to last longer than thirty seconds.

The flame flickered near the damp wood. The cross swarmed with thousands of tiny insects, and they scattered as the fire neared. Courtney unzipped his fly and slid her hand inside his jeans. He looked at her, but she was staring at the lighter in anticipation.

Is she a pyromaniac or something?

Her fingers closed around his dick and he no longer cared.

The lighter wavered beside the cross, but it refused to catch. He pressed it up against the wood and the flame fizzled out.

'Come on,' she said. 'Burn it...burn it...'

He tried again, but the lighter wouldn't work. Unwilling to remove his hand from Courtney's breast, he tried a final time, and dropped the lighter. It landed somewhere in the dirt.

'Shit.'

He bent to search for it, scrabbling through the forest floor, determined to light this fucking cross if it was the last thing he ever did. He wanted Courtney, more than he had ever wanted anything or anyone before.

'Where the fuck is it?' he muttered, as above him the cross erupted in a burst of lunatic flame.

Courtney jumped backwards, tripping and landing on her ass.

'Oh my god,' she breathed, and in the light of the fire, Steve could see she was smiling.

'I never even touched it,' he said, watching the flames lick higher, reaching for the sky in their mad dance. His hands found the lighter half-buried in the heather. He picked it up and stared at it. 'I swear, I...I never—'

'Hey,' said Courtney. She sat on the ground, staring at him. 'You gonna fuck me or stand there stuttering?'

Steve was surprised at how difficult that decision was to make.

~

'It has to be them,' said Grady.

'What, you think Steve brought a candle?' said Beth. 'He's Mr Romantic all of a sudden?'

'Well, someone brought it.'

He was right. She swung the torchlight towards the ruined structure. The ceiling was long gone, but the graffiti-coated walls remained intact. GRADY 4 BETH 4EVA read one missive, scrawled by Grady himself, so many years ago that it may as well have been a past life. A birch tree grew from inside, its skeletal limbs stretching to the stars. In the soft light of the moon, the tree seemed to glow.

'Someone must live here,' said Grady.

'Who?'

'I don't know,' he whispered. 'Maybe a woodland wildman.'

'A what?'

Grady shrugged. 'It could be.'

She looked at him, wondering whether to tell him there was no such thing as a woodland wildman. The candle glimmered lazily in the window. 'Steve?' she called out. 'You in there?'

Not even the wind blew in response.

'It's not Steve,' said Grady, failing to disguise the tremor in his voice.

Beth nudged him. 'Go check it out.'

'The fuck I will.'

They waited, their breaths misting the air. She hadn't realised how cold it was until now.

'Is anyone there?' shouted Beth.

Leaves rustled nearby, and she spun, the torch alighting a patch of stinging nettles and nothing else.

'Beth?' said Grady.

'Yeah?'

'Where did the candle go?'

She turned back to the cottage and found it in darkness. Without knowing why, she took a step forwards. Something was calling her, urging her to come closer. There were no words, but she felt it in the pit of her stomach.

'Oh to hell with this,' said Grady. 'Let's go wait in the van. If those two are having sex, we won't have to wait long.'

'How do *you* know?' said Beth, grateful for the distraction of salacious gossip.

'I slept in the same room as Steve after one of Niall's parties. He had a girl with him. I think it was Annette, remember her? Anyway, it was all over in about twenty seconds.'

'Who's Annette?'

'You know, tall girl, big...look, it doesn't matter. Let's just get out of here.'

Beth knew he was right, and yet still something called to her, a strange siren song that only she could hear. She had a powerful feeling that if she didn't investigate the cottage, she would regret it for the rest of her life.

'I'm going to go look,' she decided, giving in to her instincts, the wind guiding her onwards.

'Beth, don't. There's beer in the van. And a radio.' Grady paused. 'And it's warm.'

She handed him the torch. 'Take it. Head back if you like. But I'm going in.'

'C'mon, Beth. Really?'

She nodded. 'Aren't you curious?' She took his hand. 'Don't you want some excitement for once?'

'Yeah, but—'

'Then let's go.' She looked him in the eyes, tried to smile.

'It's just a candle in a window. What's the worst that could happen?'

'We could walk in on Steve and Courtney having a three-some with a woodland wildman,' said Grady, and Beth laughed.

'I hear that,' she said, and together they walked through the long grass towards Maggie's cottage, feeling as close to each other as they had in months.

The cross on Maggie's grave burned with disquieting intensity, illuminating the young lovers below it and nothing else. Even the trees appeared to retreat from the feverish blaze, their branches turned up, their trunks angled away.

Sweat dripped down Steve's brow as Courtney looked up at him with wide eyes, her lips parted. He started to crouch, but she waved an admonishing finger at him.

'Wait,' she said.

Steve did as he was told.

She unbuttoned the rest of the fasteners on her shirt and rested on her elbows, the garment opening, held in place by her breasts.

'Like what you see?'

He nodded too eagerly, like a dog waiting for its owner to throw a stick.

Courtney smiled as she unbuckled her belt, followed by the big brass button on her jeans.

'You can help, if you like,' she said, leaning back and letting her hair cascade over her shoulders. Sometimes, in the sparkle of the fire, she still looked like Courtney, but other times the flickering embers would catch her face in a new light, and she appeared different. It only lasted a second at a time, and Steve, being Steve, blamed the alcohol. Well, what else could it be? He felt absurdly drunk, or high, or something like that. His shoulder twitched in anticipation, his penis bulging as he knelt before her, slipping his fingers into the waistband of her jeans and tugging them down, trying to do it slowly so as not to ruin the moment.

'My panties too,' she said.

Steve had never heard anyone say that word in real life. In Scotland they were just pants or knickers, and hearing it drove him mad with desire.

She raised her ass from the ground to assist him, then sat back down as Steve stripped her jeans and underwear off, laying them on the grass beside her. He was sweating. They were too close to the fire.

That's no ordinary fire. That's a burning cross.

Man, that was bad. If there was a hell, he definitely had a one-way ticket. Courtney smiled up at him and pulled her shirt open.

But what a way to go, right?

He hauled his own shirt over his head, so fast that he forgot to suck his belly in, then stood, hastily unbuckling his jeans and shimmying out of them. The jeans were too tight, and he tripped, shooting out a hand to arrest his fall. He was heading for the cross, but his flailing hands grabbed the stones near the top.

The pyramid was icy cold to the touch.

It made no sense. It was right next to a raging inferno. He looked at his hand. There were no marks on it, no scalding, no—

'Hey,' said Courtney, sounding annoyed. 'I'm down here, asshole.'

'Huh? Oh, yeah.'

He tried to forget about it, which was easy to do.

Courtney opened her legs, and he knelt between them. She looked different again. There was a brief sparkle of cruelty in her eyes, her face changing, and then it was gone and she was Courtney once more.

She ran her tongue over her lips and reached down between her thighs. 'Are you gonna fuck me on top of this witch, or not?' she said.

It was not a sentence Steve had expected to hear today. He put one hand on Courtney's waist, the other on his dick, and guided himself in.

Courtney — or the other woman, the one who lived behind her face — welcomed him with a smile.

Beth approached the cottage, Grady trailing after her with the torch.

She was glad he was accompanying her, even though it was clear he didn't want to be. Could she blame him? Not really. Cook's Point at night always had an odd atmosphere. Even as a kid, she remembered finding it hard to drift off to sleep in the tent. There were too many strange noises, too many sudden drops in temperature. It didn't help that she usually shared a tent with Alice, who had been a remarkably highly strung child, seeing figures in shadows and hearing voices where there were none. Still, she couldn't ignore the unusual sensation that flowed through her veins, a desire — no, a *need* — to go further, to investigate.

The grass was up to her knees, soaking through her trousers. She hadn't planned on traipsing through a forest when she had left the house that afternoon. It should have been a typical Saturday night of bowling and drinking until she no longer felt that aching sense of ennui.

Now, here she was — *Beth Collins, Ghosthunter!*

She paused at the doorway. Despite the moonlight, and the lack of a roof, the interior was pitch black. Rather than wait for Grady to arrive with the torch, she took a deep breath, dipped her head — people in the olden days must have been so short — and stepped inside the ruined building. Strange things crunched underfoot. They were probably twigs, but the delicate way they crackled made them sound like eggs. She stood motionless, waiting for her eyes to adjust to the darkness.

'Grady, you coming?' she said, her vision returning. She could make out the walls, and an old stone fireplace, but above her? Nothing.

Moon must be behind the clouds, she thought. Funny, it hadn't been this dark in the clearing. She looked up at the obsidian blackness above her, feeling oddly claustrophobic. No moon, no stars, no clouds.

Nothing.

'Grady?'

He didn't answer, and suddenly she wanted out.

She looked around the room, but couldn't find the doorway. Stumbling forwards, she tripped over her own feet and landed on her knees, shattering the egg-like objects that carpeted the ground. But by then, she already knew they weren't eggs.

They were skulls.

Hundreds and hundreds of tiny human skulls.

'Oh god,' she said, her heart hammering against her ribcage. 'Oh fuck.'

She stood, crushing the barely developed bones beneath the soles of her bright blue running shoes, and ran for where she thought the exit should be, thumping into a heavy wooden door.

What door? There wasn't one a second ago...

She tried to suck in a breath, but none would come. A light flickered behind her, and her own shadow moved across the wall like some creeping horror. She twirled around, hands clenching into fists. A small flame twinkled over by the far wall.

The candle.

It moved through the air, not quite bright enough to illuminate its carrier's face.

'Steve?' she choked. 'Courtney?'

The figure stopped and turned its body towards her. It raised the candle, infinitesimally slowly, towards its head. Beth turned back to the door, searching for a handle, a way out. She didn't want to see who was in here with her, because she knew that if she saw its face — its gruesome, appalling face — then she would surely lose her mind.

There was no door, there was no door.

The thought rippled over and over.

It can't be real. None of this is real.

She placed both palms against the wood, closing her eyes, wishing the nightmare away.

Something pounded on the other side, the door shaking from the furious impact. Beth screamed. She couldn't help it.

The door rattled in its frame.

'What the fuck?' she cried. 'Steve, if that's you, I'll fucking kill you.' She didn't recognise her own voice. It sounded different, older.

Thump thump thump.

The knocking persisted, building in intensity.

Against her better judgement, she glanced over her shoulder. The figure had vanished, and candles were lit all around the interior of the cottage — on the mantel, lining the walls. The fireplace, which had been cold and unused moments before, now roared, a metal pot hanging above it, liquid bubbling within.

'*Come out, Maggie. You know why we're here.*'

Beth backed up until she thudded into the wall. A couple of the candles fell to the floor.

'Stop it! Please!'

'*Come quietly, Maggie. For the sake of your soul, come on out.*'

'I'm not Maggie!' she screamed, tears streaming down her face. She dropped to her knees, unwittingly crushing a child's skull. 'Leave me alone!'

The knocking stopped, replaced by the dismal wail of the wind. Was there a lonelier sound on Earth?

Beth got to her feet, wiping the tears from her eyes. The candles seemed to lead her on, the walls closing in at impossible angles. Once at the door, she pressed her ear to it, hearing nothing but the wind. Then even that stopped. It was a silence beyond silence, an oppressive nothingness, the lack of basic natural order. She hadn't gone deaf — her heart beat noisily, and she swore she could hear her own blood rushing through her veins — but other than that, she was in a vacuum.

Groping for the door handle, she found instead a sliding wooden latch and dragged it back. The wooden door swung open, but there was nothing to see, the cottage floating in an uncanny black void. The darkness seemed to invite her into its callous embrace, and she stepped backwards.

Then hands grabbed her, gripping her shoulders, her head, forcing her down onto the bed of skulls that cracked and stabbed their rotten splinters into her back.

'*Foul creature! Ungodly wench! May the full wrath of the Lord strike you down!*'

'I'm not her!' she cried, but something entered her mouth, heavy and metal and rusted, pressing against her tongue, her teeth cracking off the ghastly device as it plunged further into her throat.

'*Pray silence,*' said a man she couldn't see. '*You shall not mock the Lord with your dev'lish tongue!*'

Beth gagged, vomit spilling out the sides of her mouth.

Unable to move, she lay in the darkness as feet paced around her in a wide arc. They stopped, and a voice, old and thunderous and not-of-this-Earth, spoke.

'*In the name of God...look at her. Is she with child?*'

13

STEVE KISSED COURTNEY AND THOUGHT OF BORIS JOHNSON.

It was an old trick, one he used to prolong his state of arousal. Anytime he felt near release — like *right...this... second* — he pictured the potato-faced clown waving a Union Flag and grinning.

'It's working,' he grunted.

'Huh?' said Courtney.

Steve didn't reply. He nibbled her ear, then moved his head to her breasts, running his tongue over her nipples.

The Johnson trick was infallible. He had first tried it by thinking of his own mother, which is what Bobby Murdo had told him to do when they were fifteen-year-old virgins, but that had almost ruined sex for him forever. He found it worked best with politicians. David Cameron, Theresa May, take your pick. They were all tremendous erection killers.

They should put that on their business cards, he thought, and smiled, his hands cradling Courtney's ass, squeezing it.

'Stop fucking grinning,' she said. 'You look like an idiot.'

He ignored the comment. 'You on the pill?'

'Little fucking late to ask,' she said, wincing at his clumsy movements. 'Just shut up and fuck me.'

Steve needed no encouragement. He looked into her eyes, but she was gazing past him, up at the grave, at the wild flames that cast bizarre shadows, their entwined bodies shapeless and otherworldly.

Boris Johnson on a zip wire, Boris Johnson on a zip wire.

She panted, moaning softly, her gaze never leaving the blazing holy symbol that towered over them. She dug her nails into his skin, thrusting her hips with a vigour equal to his own.

'Oh god,' she said. 'That's it, that's it!'

Steve's pulse was out of control. He felt a surge between his legs.

Theresa May dancing, Theresa May dancing, Theresa May dancing.

But it wasn't working, not this time.

'I'm gonna come,' groaned Steve, desperate not to go to his last resort, which involved David Cameron and a pig's head.

'Don't you fucking dare, Pete,' said Courtney. 'Don't you fucking *dare* come without me.'

'My name's Steve,' he grunted.

'Just a little longer,' she said. Did she need more time, or was she talking about his dick? The thought killed his mood for a moment. Good! He needed all the help he could get.

'You're the best,' he said. 'Oh Courtney, you're the best ever.'

'Call me Maggie. Fuck me and call me Maggie!'

Maggie! What a brilliant idea. He pictured Margaret Thatcher in a corset, smacking a riding crop off her bare thighs and leaving a thin red welt. He was horrified to discover it wasn't enough.

'Oh god, I'm coming,' he moaned, shoving Thatcher out of his thoughts and looking down at Courtney's breasts.

'Don't come without me,' she warned. 'I'm almost there.'

'I won't, I won't, I...*shit!*'

He let go of her ass and put his hands in the dirt on either side of her face, his limbs tensing up.

'What's wrong now?' said Courtney, her hips still grinding against his pelvis. 'Did you—'

'No,' he yelped, in a high-pitched whine he hadn't used since his voice had broken. His body spasmed.

'You fucking did, you little shit,' she said.

But he was telling the truth. He hadn't come, not yet.

'I...ow! Fuck!' He took several sharp intakes of breath as Courtney glared up at him, a thin sheen of sweat on her glowing face.

'Jesus Christ, you look like you're taking a shit,' she spat. 'Get off me you fucking jerk, I'll finish myself off.'

'I can't,' he panted, tears in his confused and frightened eyes. 'I'm...oh shit, Courtney. I think I'm *stuck*.'

'She carries the antichrist!'

The voice came from deep inside her own head. Beth could see no one, and yet something pinned her to the ground, holding her wrists and ankles in a death-grip.

'Disrobe the devil's whore. She must be cleansed!'

She wanted to scream, to shout for Grady, or Steve, or anyone, but the vile metallic instrument was lodged in her throat, the enamel of her teeth clacking off the edges. It rubbed against her tongue, tasting of copper and vomit.

There was a tearing sound as her jacket split up the seams, invisible hands ripping it from her body. She shook in helpless terror at the spectral assault. The stitching on her trousers tore up the sides of both legs, almost lifting her from the ground, and her sweater stretched and burst open. Fingers cold with the touch of death grabbed at her. She heard the elastic on her underwear snap, the fabric shredding.

I'm not her, she wanted to scream. *I'm not Maggie! I'm Beth Collins!*

Instead, she wept as dark, shapeless fingers thrust between her legs, invading her body with intimate savagery.

'Aye, tis true. She carries Satan's seed.'

'Then for the sake of all that is holy...cut it out. In the name of the Lord, cut it out of her!'

Suddenly she could see them, a group of ten or twelve men, faces wild with resentment and fury and unbridled horror. They held her legs, her arms, her head. Two of them clutched crucifixes, their brows soaked in perspiration. They parted to allow access to a bearded man wearing a loose cloth sack tied at the waist with frayed rope. He dragged a sword behind him, the metal scraping off the floor with an anxious screech.

Beth's blood ran cold.

'Hold her still,' he said, looking skyward. *'And may God forgive me.'*

'What do you mean, *stuck*? You're inside me!'

'I'm fucking stuck,' shouted Steve, the panic rising. 'I can't get out!'

He pushed himself up, muscles straining, and took Courtney with him.

'Oh what the fuck!' she screamed as her ass left the ground. 'What's wrong with you? Put me down!'

'It's your fault! You're...too tight,' wailed Steve. 'Are you a virgin?'

'Oh, fuck off and get off me,' she said. 'I knew I shoulda fucked the other guy.'

Steve reached for the shaft of his penis. He was, as he liked to describe it to Grady, *balls deep*. A dread unlike any he had ever experienced took hold. He kept thinking, *what if we have to go to the hospital like this?*

I'm sorry, the doctors would tell his mother. *The penis had to be surgically removed. But don't worry, we've kept it in a jar for you.*

'I'm going to try to pull it out,' he said with a shaky voice.

'Do it, just get it out of me!'

'It hurts,' groaned Steve. He was ashamed to realise he was weeping. 'It hurts so bad.'

'Well don't fucking *cry* about it.'

He slid his fingers along his slippery member until he came to Courtney's vagina, and forced them in.

'Jesus, hurry up,' she said, scowling at him in discomfort.

'I'm trying,' sobbed Steve. What was happening? What was stopping his—

Wait. What was *that*?

'Ow,' said Courtney as Steve probed deeper. 'You're hurting me you fucking asshole.'

'I'm caught on something,' he said.

'Oh yeah, I forgot I left a fucking *bear trap* in there.'

'Just shut up,' he said. 'I've almost got it.' His fingers touched something. It was wrapped around his penis like a cock ring. Was it one of those birth control devices he had heard about? What was that one...the coil? Steve imagined it to be a like a spring, or a small Slinky. Could that be what he was caught on?

'Hey, that fucking hurts!' said Courtney, spittle flying from her lips.

'Me too,' he said. Whatever was on his dick was clinching harder, the pain immense. He traced his finger around it, searching for a way to free himself, and found a ragged bump. What was it? There was another alongside it. Courtney squirmed, her face screwed up in agony.

'Keep still,' said Steve. 'I'm caught on...'

'On *what?*'

'I don't know,' he said, breaking down and hyperventilating. He probed deeper. 'What have you got in there?' he wailed, tracing his fingers over whatever he was snagged on, discovering a small, hardened shell at the tip.

Only then did he realise.

That wasn't a shell...it was a fingernail. The bumps were knuckles.

'Oh Jesus,' he said. *'Oh Jesus fucking Christ!'*

He felt the ragged nails pressing into his penis.

'Steve, get your fucking dick out of me right this fucking instant!' screamed Courtney.

But he couldn't.

He wanted to, but Maggie Wall was holding on too tight.

Beth tried to kick out, to free herself, to wriggle free of the diabolical hands that held her, but their grip was unshakeable.

The bearded man shuffled closer. He lifted the sword and rested it on her pallid stomach.

'Do it,' said one of the holy men. *'It is the will of God.'*

He raised the weapon, the tip gleaming in the candlelight.

It's just a dream, it's just a dream, she thought.

But when she looked into the man's eyes, she knew it wasn't.

She was about to die.

'Oh god, it hurts!' cried Steve, his teardrops falling onto Courtney's own agonised face. The hand inside her squeezed his now-limp dick, harder and harder, tugging on it like it was trying to pull him into Courtney cock-first. The skin around his groin stretched, becoming almost translucent, thin paper-cut holes opening and growing longer. Courtney kicked him ferociously, the pain within mounting with each passing second, her insides pressing together.

'Ugh!' squeaked Steve, as his penis ripped from his body. He hurled himself backwards, thick black blood oozing from the torn stump.

Courtney writhed in the grass, clutching her hands over her vagina, blood gushing from it. Steve watched as she arched her back, lit only by the blazing cross of Maggie's grave. He was going to vomit or pass out, whichever came first.

When the gnarled, blood-soaked hand of Maggie Wall appeared from between Courtney's legs, he did both.

Steve fell backwards into the dirt, jets of blood issuing from the tattered mess of his crotch. He swam in and out of consciousness, until he was no longer sure if what he was seeing was fantasy or reality.

Courtney's body shuddered unnaturally, her belly rippling and stretching, legs kicking wildly. One arm, long and grey and withered, extended out from between her thighs, grasping at thin air, the greying, cracked skin drenched in blood that dripped from sharpened nails.

A second arm appeared, splitting Courtney up to her navel, and she expired in a welter of blood-drenched screams. From inside her — from deep, *deep* inside her — Steve thought he saw a pair of eyes watching him with ghoulish interest. Below them gleamed rows of white teeth.

Whatever it was, it looked like it was smiling.

Beth steeled herself, preparing for the worst.

She waited.

Then, she waited some more.

After a while she got tired of waiting and opened her eyes. Far above her, the stars twinkled dolefully. She reached one arm up towards them as if in a dream. The roof of the cottage was gone again, the moon slithering out from behind the clouds and bathing the interior in soft pools of mellow light. The men, too, had disappeared, and she was all alone. She patted herself down, finding her clothes intact, then curled into a ball on the soft bed of pine needles.

Skulls. These were skulls.

No. That had been a nightmare, an illusion. Her heart slowed, gradually returning to normal. When her legs lost their rubbery feeling, she forced herself to stand. Her cheeks were wet with tears, and she could still taste vomit in the back of her throat. As quickly as she could manage, Beth exited Maggie's dwelling and fell to her knees in the long dewy grass. The last thing she remembered was that dreadful implement hovering above her, ready to strike, to cut her open.

She instinctively pressed her legs together, and thought she might vomit again. When the nausea passed she got unsteadily to her feet, feet that moments before had been held by—

Those feet weren't yours, the irrational — or was it rational? — part of her mind said. *They belonged to Maggie Wall.*

'No,' she said, running frozen hands down her face. 'It's not possible.'

But she knew it was. It was no dream, and she had never felt more sober in her life. Beth shivered. The clearing was empty. Where was everybody? How much time had elapsed? A dry wind wrapped around her, whipping her breath away.

'Grady?'

There was no answer. Beady eyes watched her from the trees, catching the moonlight and then darting out of sight. She thought she heard something, a strangulated yelp that sounded like Steve, and staggered towards the sound, avoiding the cottage. It no longer called to her the way it had before. She needed to get back home, to the safety of her bed.

Harsh yellow light flickered through the woods ahead.

A fire.

Thank god!

They were still here. Feeling more in control, Beth sped up. Every tree trunk she touched, every fern that brushed past her skin, made her feel better. It had all been a dream, a dark and perverted dream. She wanted to call out again, but something prevented her, a sense of unease from the darkest recesses of her mind. The fire was too high, almost as if it floated above the ground.

No, that wasn't it.

It was the cross.

The cross atop Maggie's grave, that had stood for over three-hundred years, was on fire. Despite the heat, her spine tingled. She stepped out of the foliage, the clearing lit up like Guy Fawkes Night, and froze, her world careening out of balance. She almost fell, catching a branch with her trailing fingers, holding herself steady.

Steve lay a few feet from the grave. He was naked, crimson fluid bubbling from the wreckage between his legs, coating his thighs and belly. His eyes were wide and milky white, staring sightlessly into the beyond.

But it was what was happening to Courtney that really flipped the switch to insanity. Beth watched as a jagged grey tree sprouted forth between the American girl's legs. Her body had been torn up to her ribcage, her legs jutting out at absurd angles. Stringy intestines dangled mockingly from the branches of the tree, blood pooling beneath it.

When it turned to look at her, Beth almost lost her grip.

It wasn't a tree, it was a person — grotesquely emaciated, limbs perished and distorted, with a round, wrinkled face like mouldy fruit perched atop a sinuous neck.

It was coming out of Courtney, dragging itself free from her body.

Beth backed away, shaking her head senselessly.

Then the burning cross extinguished itself and plunged the clearing into darkness.

14

TIME PASSED SLOWLY IN JAIL.

Alice had only been in the cell for an hour at most, but it felt like a lifetime. How did prisoners manage it? How did they cope with the lack of freedom, the absence of space? She paced back and forth, placing both hands on the dusty bars and pushing herself away, over and over.

Where was Eric? If Carlisle was telling the truth, she'd be seeing him soon. And then what? He had killed her mum, stolen her baby...how far would he go to cover up his crimes?

The cell had the luxury of a small, barred window to which she frequently returned. Her mum used to tell her that windows were nature's television, which was such a mum thing to say, but it made sense to her now. What a pity there was nothing worth watching tonight. Auchenmullan was a ghost town as usual. One time she heard a car, but when she got to the window, it had passed. Two trees blocked most of the view — a particularly evil piece of gardening — but the mountain could be seen between them in all its shadowy glory.

She heard the station doors open, and a muffled discussion taking place. A woman's voice, reassuringly familiar. Was it Beth's mum? It sounded like her. Alice moved to the corner closest to the door, but it made little difference. Her legs were tired, and she sat on the edge of the bed and looked down at her feet. The mattress was uncomfortably solid, but the only other place to sit was a filthy-looking toilet, and she wasn't going anywhere near *that*. Well, not until she had to. Damn, why did she have to pee so often these days?

She thought of Eric. He must be so scared. Well, maybe scared wasn't the right word, but he would know something was wrong.

He needs me. He needs his mum.

It was every parent's worst nightmare. Separated from her child by a madman. She began to question her worth as a mother. Why had she gone out two days in a row? Did she not love him enough? Was she too immature, too childish? Did she not deserve happiness?

She cried for a while, feeling useless and alone and scared, her mind continuing to wander down paths better left untrodden.

What if Carlisle is going to kill him? What if he's already—

No. She mustn't think that, for it would mean she had nothing left to live for.

Footsteps thundered down the hall. The visitor was gone, and Carlisle was coming back. The doors opened, and there he was, carrying a white bundle in his arms. Alice leapt to her feet and ran towards him, poking her arms through the bars like a zombie searching for its prey.

'Eric!' she shouted, eyes wide with desperation.

'No,' he said. 'Not yet.'

Deflated, she rested her head hopelessly against the bars, letting her arms drop. 'Why are you doing this to me?'

'You won't understand,' he said wearily, 'but you'll find out soon enough.' He shoved the bundle of white fabric into her hands. 'Here, put this on.'

She regarded him through the bars. 'What?'

'Take it and put it on. That's an order.'

She pulled the fabric into the cell. It was clothing of some sort. She held the garment up and it unravelled, reaching the floor. A white cotton dress with red trim, six chunky brown buttons down the middle. Judging by the wonky hemline, the outfit had been hurriedly stitched together.

'What the fuck is this?' she said.

'Show some respect,' he snapped. 'Mrs Collins tried her best. She spent all morning...ach, just put it on, and be quick about it.'

Alice shoved the garment back through the bars, letting it fall at Carlisle's boots. 'I'm not wearing this. Not until you bring me Eric.'

Carlisle seethed, colour creeping into his cheeks. 'I think you *will* wear it. Because if you do, you'll get to *see* your baby.' He shrugged in an attempt at nonchalance. 'It's up to you.'

They stared at each other, then Carlisle bent and picked up the dress.

She snatched it from him.

Did she believe a word he said? Not at all, but what choice did she have? Better to play along for now. There was nothing she could do while trapped in this damn prison cell.

Under the watchful eye of Inspector Carlisle, she lifted the dress over her head and—

'No,' barked Carlisle. 'Take the rest off first.'

She looked at him for a long time. 'What?'

He looked away. 'Just the dress. Nothing else.' Then, sheepishly, he added, 'I'm sorry. It's the rules.'

She wanted to question him further, but it was pointless. The dress, the rules...it was all bullshit.

You know what to do. Play along.

'If I do,' she said, 'you'll take me to Eric?'

'I swear to God.'

She nodded. 'Okay. But turn around.' He started to protest, and she interrupted. 'It's not like I can run away, is it?'

'Fine,' he said impatiently, turning his back on her. 'But be quick.'

She kicked off her shoes and hurriedly disrobed, leaving her jacket, leggings and jumper on the bed, but keeping her underwear on. The dress was ill-fitting, and hung baggily over her like the world's ugliest wedding dress, displaying far more cleavage than Alice was normally comfortable showing.

'Okay, done,' she said. 'Can I put my shoes back on?'

He turned, running appraising eyes over her and smiling a satisfied smile. 'You look fine. It was short notice, but it'll have to do.'

'And my shoes?'

'No shoes,' he said. 'You won't need them.'

'What's going on?' she asked one last time.

'Be patient. It won't be long.'

'That doesn't answer my question.'

'No,' he said. 'I suppose it doesn't.'

She thought of Eric again. A tear trickled down her cheek, and she shuffled to the window, unwilling to let Carlisle see her cry. The floor was cold against her bare feet, and she looked up at Cook's Point, wondering if her friends were there, and what they were doing. Would she be dead by the time they came back? What if she never got a chance to say goodbye?

The cell door unlocked, and Carlisle entered. She heard him, but didn't turn round.

Something had caught her eye.

She felt Carlisle's hand on her shoulder.

'Time to go,' he said. She didn't reply. 'Hey, I'm talking to you. You want to see your wee one, or not?'

'Yeah,' she said absently, not taking her eyes from the mountain.

Carlisle was growing impatient. 'What are you looking at, lassie?'

'There's a fire up there,' she said in a dreamy, disbelieving voice.

Carlisle barged into her, almost knocking her over, and looked at the small blaze about three-quarters of the way up the mountain, near Cook's Point. They stood together, captor and captive, watching the strange yellow light that glowed like a lighthouse.

'It doesn't seem real,' said Alice. Carlisle grabbed her by the arm and hauled her out of the cell and down the corridor before she had time to protest.

'Come on,' he said. 'We have to hurry.' Then, to himself, he muttered, 'It's happening. Mother of God, *it's happening again.*'

15

GRADY WAS WORRIED.

No, that was the understatement of the century.

He was scared *shitless*.

The door to the van was unlocked, but there was no trace of Beth. She wasn't in the back either. The extra beers were there, the mirror ball hanging motionless from the roof. It was exactly as they had left it.

Where the hell *was* she?

Beth had been right in front of him as they headed for the cottage, and that goddam freaky candle. Then a noise had made him turn his head, a howl unlike anything he'd heard before, even deep in the woods. Shining the light into the foliage, he had seen nothing, and when he turned back, Beth was gone. He had called out her name, jogging towards the cottage, keeping the beam locked on the entrance. She wasn't inside. There were beer cans so rusted they were impossible to identify, and the remains of a crude campfire, but by the looks of it, no one had been inside Maggie's cottage for years. Beth had simply...vanished.

There was only one reasonable explanation — she had

gone back to the van without him. He couldn't understand why, but it was more logical than her going to watch Steve and Courtney shagging. So Grady had made his way through the woods, along the old trail, following the markers, his fear increasing with each nervous step.

Now he sat in the van, trying to figure out his next move. Where else could she have gone? She must be lost. He decided to signal to her, give her a sound to follow. The forest was thick, almost impenetrable at points, and dangerous at night. There was marshland and loose rocks and fallen trees.

And witches.

No, not witches. That was ridiculous.

Grady jabbed the horn on the steering wheel, but much like the rest of the old van, it was only good for comic effect. A low, flatulent *parp* escaped the vehicle. He tried again, the second attempt producing nothing but a steady hiss of air.

'Shit,' he said, thumping his fist off the wheel. What now? Go back out and search, or wait for her to turn up? How could Beth have disappeared...she was only out of his sight for two or three seconds at most?

The radio.

Yes, that was it. The horn didn't work, but if he could get the radio loud enough, that would act as a sort-of beacon for Beth to follow. It didn't matter that Grady had no keys, as the van didn't actually have an inbuilt car-radio. That would be too 20th Century for Steve's dad. Instead, a small battery-operated radio was gaffer taped to the dashboard, in what amounted to the crudest bit of DIY Grady had ever seen. It was right over where the passenger airbag would open, the unlucky recipient destined to receive a faceful of chunky metal in the event of an accident. It was why Grady and Beth always refused to ride alongside Steve in the rickety old death-trap. He twiddled the dials, picking up nothing but static.

In the safety of the van, he felt like an idiot. So there had been a candle in the window...so what? What did he think, that the place was haunted? He had been up here dozens of times as a kid, and inside Maggie's cottage on most of those occasions.

Never at night, though. Things are different at night, when the sun goes down and the spirits come out.

It did no good to think like that. He looked out the windscreen. Ahead lay Auchenmullan, and beyond that, on a clear day, the Cairngorm mountains. If he squinted, he could just about make out their outline, like distant phantoms hovering over the town. He checked the wing-mirror for a sign of Beth, but even the trees were still. The radio buzzed and screeched but found no station, and he switched it off.

Had she run away from him? Maybe she just wanted some time to herself, time to think. He knew they were about to break up. Or maybe they already had? Grady was no fool, he had seen it coming, but like her, he wasn't ready to admit it. He loved Beth, and wanted to be with her, but only if she wanted the same, and it was clear she no longer did.

Does she want to break up with you, or with Auchenmullan?

What was the difference? In January, Grady was due to start work at the car dealership his father worked at in Inverness. He had enquired about getting Beth a job there, and they said they were looking for a part-time secretary. He hadn't told her about it yet.

Fuck, he really *was* turning into his parents.

He opened the door and stepped outside into the chill night air, gazing into the thick morass of pine and birch trees. Someone was coming, he was sure of it. The wind picked up, swaying the ferns, and whipping up mini tornadoes of pine needles. The air felt different. *Humid*, almost. He mopped his brow with his jacket sleeve. It was impossible — it could be no more than five degrees up here. Hell, his breath clouded in front of his face with each exhalation. He breathed in, the unmistakable scent of burning pine filling his nostrils.

Steve must have built a fire. Were they all sitting around it together, wondering where he was? They were probably laughing about it.

'Fuck it,' he said, his mind made up. He would venture back out to look for her. Closing the door, he started up the path, feeling strangely reassured. He shouldn't have panicked. He'd never hear the end of it, especially from Steve, who would delight in slagging him off in front of Courtney. Grady didn't care. He had no interest in the American girl. All he had hoped to do was make Beth jealous, provoke a reaction from her to see if she still cared.

The air grew thicker, hotter, and he wished he wasn't wearing his jacket, which was ridiculous. It was October in the Scottish Highlands, and it looked like it might snow at any moment. It should be freezing cold and pissing it down.

An idea hit him.

The beer!

Ha! If he turned up with the remaining six packs, Steve might go easy on him. *Never insult the man who brings you beer,* Steve liked to say, usually referring to Jack back at the alley.

Pleased with himself, Grady trudged to the van, taking his jacket off and throwing it in, wedging himself between the front seats to access the alcohol. It was just out of reach, and he stretched his arm out, fingertips brushing the cardboard packaging.

'Come on,' he muttered, and then something slammed against the passenger window with an almighty *crack*. Grady screamed and tried to spin onto his back without getting stuck between the seats. He looked at the window and, for a moment, thought he was staring at a giant spider perched on its web.

It was a hand, the miniature cracks in the glass spiralling out to the edges of the frame.

The hand withdrew, the door opened, and Beth scrambled into the van, her face as pale as the moon. She looked at Grady wedged between the seats, and said, *'Go, go, we gotta go now!'*

'Beth, are you—' he started, but she cut him off.

'Drive!' she screamed. 'We have to go!'

He disentangled himself from the seats. 'We're not going anywhere until you—'

She grabbed his arm, her fingers pressing into his flesh with a maniac's grip. 'Don't you see? Don't you understand? *She killed them.* She's back. I don't know how, I don't know why, I—'

'What the fuck have you taken?' snapped Grady.

Confusion set in on Beth's face, her eyes wide and unblinking. 'What? Nothing. I had, like, a vision or something, I don't know, I was...'

She spoke so fast Grady struggled to keep up.

'What did Courtney give you?' he said. 'LSD? Coke? Where's Steve?'

Beth was shivering violently, beads of sweat running down her face. She tried to slow down. 'I didn't take anything, I swear. I saw Maggie Wall...she killed them. She killed them both. She was coming out of...out of...oh fuck, she was...'

Grady stared at her, not knowing what to do. 'Listen,' he said, trying unsuccessfully to sound calm. 'Everything's going to be okay. You've taken something, but you're safe now, and everything's going to be fine.'

'It's not, Grady, aren't you listening? She killed them both, and she'll be coming for us next. She was almost—'

She stopped mid-sentence, her head jerking to the side, an expression of utter terror frozen on her face.

'She's coming.'

'Beth, you need to calm down,' he said, but he didn't feel calm himself, not in the slightest. She was freaking him out. 'I'm gonna go and get Steve, and then—'

'No,' she said. 'Please, don't go. We have to get off the mountain, we have to get back to town.'

'And we will,' he said, 'I promise you. But Steve's got the keys.'

Her face fell. Grady took her hand and squeezed it.

'Without Steve, we're not going anywhere. You understand that, don't you?'

She stared vacantly out the window. 'Then we're going to die.'

Grady had no reply. He had never seen Beth like this. *Never.* She was crazy, her wild eyes darting around, refusing to settle. Her hands trembled. She was on drugs, alright. No doubt about it. He had to find Steve and get him to drive them home, even if it meant interrupting him mid-coitus.

'I'm gonna go find the others,' he said. 'I won't be long.'

She didn't look at him.

'We're going to die,' she repeated.

He started to say otherwise, then decided against it. There

was no time to talk her down. It could take all night. If he had to though, he would stay up with her til morning, reassuring her that everything was okay. So what if they weren't together anymore? She was still his oldest friend. His *best* friend.

And he loved her.

Grady opened the door and got out. The trees shifted listlessly in a hot breeze that seemed to blow in from the fucking Sahara. He took a last look at Beth. Her body was limp, slumped in the seat, and he wanted to go to her, hold her, comfort her.

There'll be plenty of time for that. For now, she needs water. She needs her bed.

He decided to take her to one of the abandoned properties, so her parents wouldn't see her in this state. There was one on Beechwood Drive, a nice place where their friend Trevor used to live. After the family had moved, Grady and Beth had used the place as a love-nest for a while. They even kept a change of clothes there. They hadn't used it for a while, but it was a secure environment, and one Beth knew. It seemed the best—

What was that?

Something moved between the trees, a splinter of dull silver glinting in the moonlight.

'Steve?' he said, though he knew it wasn't.

He took a cautious step forwards and saw it again, a fleeting glance.

It was getting closer.

His fingers fumbled for the door handle, opened it slightly.

'Beth,' he said softly. 'There's something out there.'

'It's her,' she said. She looked at him with haunted sorrow in her eyes. 'It's Maggie Wall.'

'Maggie Wall's been dead for three-hundred years,' he

said, so quietly he wasn't even sure he had spoken out loud. He closed the door again, and then he saw it. How could he not, as it emerged from the woods like a sentient birch tree, all twisted limbs and graceless posture? It was a glimpse, but that glimpse was enough to haunt a thousand lifetimes. It moved with great speed, a surreal vision from out of Grady's most torrid nightmares, whipping its way through the trees, the branches snapping like cartilage.

He felt hands on him, dragging him into the van.

Beth.

He looked at her, and she looked at him.

She had been right all along.

Maggie Wall was back, and tonight they were going to die.

16

SOMETHING HIT THE VAN FROM BEHIND. THE BACK DOORS crunched and bent, the vehicle jolting forwards a couple of inches. Beth tumbled against the dashboard.

'Get us out of here!' she yelled, as another sledgehammer blow struck the van, the wheels lifting off the ground.

Grady did nothing. He was frozen in place. The van moved again, this time to the left, the sides denting inwards, the metal crumpling as if rammed by a bulldozer.

Beth reached down to the ignition, searching for the keys, just in case...but they weren't there. They were in Steve's trouser pocket, lying next to his mutilated corpse.

She suddenly noticed the quiet. The attack had stopped. The wind whispered casual warnings through the cracked glass of the driver's window, and Beth and Grady sat in abject terror, only their breathing audible in the cramped space. Then came the footsteps, slow and methodical, circling them, and the sound of talons screeching along the metal like ancient machinery grinding into life. The thing outside tried again, smashing into the side of the van.

She's trying to find a way in, thought Beth.

She felt a hand on her knee, and jumped.

'What are we going to do?' whispered Grady.

She didn't know what to say. They were trapped. That thing outside was working its way round, and when it came to the doors, it would burst in and tear them apart, like it had done to Steve and Courtney.

Then came a voice that chilled Beth to her very marrow, one strange and sinister enough to drive the listener mad. It drawled three words, seeming to come from the bowels of the Earth itself.

'Where's...my...baby?'

Beth closed her eyes, questioning her sanity. The footsteps drew closer, nearing the passenger door, and she shuffled out of the seat, pressing into the lifeless statue of her boyfriend. Something jabbed into her arse, and for one crazed moment, she thought it was Grady. It was the handbrake.

The handbrake.

An idea came to her. Would it work? She had to try.

She clambered between the seats, landing with a thud in the back. At the sound, huge fists pounded on the exterior. She crawled over cushions and past the unopened six packs until she reached the back doors. From outside came the most godawful, unearthly shriek.

Beth balled her fists and hammered on the doors.

'Here,' she shouted. 'Come and get us!'

'Beth!' said Grady, snapping out of his funk, 'Stop! For god's sake, stop!'

The nails scratched around the van, heading for the rear. Beth continued her assault, ignoring Grady's protestations. The back doors crushed inwards as the full force of Maggie

Wall slammed into them. The van moved forwards again. Would it be enough?

'Take the handbrake off!' shouted Beth.

'What?' said Grady. 'What are you talking about?' He was panic-stricken. No, worse than that — he was *useless*.

'Fuck,' said Beth. 'I'll do it myself!'

Maggie threw herself at the doors, and they bulged inwards, a two-inch gap opening between them, and Beth saw that dreadful, horrifying face leering in at her. Maggie licked a worm-like tongue over the dried bark of her lips.

'Where's...my...baby?'

Beth scrambled between the seats again, groping wildly for the handbrake. She yanked it up as Maggie powered into the back of the van. The doors split apart, creating a gap wide enough for someone to get out...or in. Cold air invaded the vehicle, along with the fetid stink of spoiled meat, as the van lurched forwards, rolling down the hill, slowly at first, then picking up speed. Hanging half-over the seat, Beth grabbed the steering wheel, guiding the vehicle left an instant before it hit a wall of trees.

'Did we lose her?' asked Beth, her voice piercing.

Grady glanced through the broken doors. 'God, she's coming! Beth, she's chasing us!'

She didn't look back, couldn't even if she wanted to. Her eyes were fixed on the road, or what she could see of it. Without lights, they plunged forwards into an abyss, only the lunar glow guiding her as the van got faster and faster, the trees blurring past at an alarming rate.

'Help me,' sobbed Beth. 'Take the wheel.'

Grady swallowed hard and gripped the steering wheel with raw white knuckles.

'We need to slow down, or we're going to crash,' said Grady, as they sped through the darkness. The road was a simple one — it wound its way down the mountain in an endless spiral — but at the rate they were going, the vehicle was bound to lose control, especially when the trees enclosed the road again and the light all-but vanished.

Beth settled herself into the driver's seat, taking over the steering from Grady. The van buffeted over the uneven track, dirt and rocks cascading behind them. They swerved dangerously close to the lip of the road, the back wheel briefly overhanging a sheer drop. She jerked the wheel, almost jackknifing the vehicle onto its side, before it righted itself, and they continued their rollercoaster descent. She partially raised the handbrake, metal groaning against metal, and the van slowed. Releasing the brake, they picked up speed again.

'Is she still there?' asked Beth, her whole body taut.

Grady glanced over his shoulder, looking through the dented back doors.

'I can't see her.'

Beth raised the handbrake again, slowing them for a few seconds, before letting it go.

'That'll do for now,' she said, and focused on the road ahead.

Trees shot by, the tyres of the van bouncing over roots and stones as they plummeted downhill in a never-ending cycle of gaining speed and slowing down, gaining speed and slowing down. They were deep in the forest now, surrounded by darkness, and Beth flashed back to the nightmare in the cottage.

That was no nightmare.

No, she knew that now. Understood it, even. She had

been Maggie Wall, in her skin, living through her final moments, as they killed her, ransacked her body, and stole her baby. A shiver trembled the length of her spine.

'What was that?' said Grady, breaking the eerie silence.

The brakes screeched as Beth used the handbrake, then relaxed, the van rolling along at around forty. She daren't go any faster, not at night.

'That was Maggie Wall,' she said quietly.

'But it can't be.' He didn't sound convinced, and Beth chose not to argue. There was no point. Her eyes never shifted from the road. It was flattening out, which brought with it a whole new set of problems. Still, she could worry about that when the time came. For now, she would just ease off the handbrake a little.

'Why is she here?' whispered Grady.

'I don't know,' said Beth. 'She came...*out* of Courtney.' She choked back tears as she remembered the vivid scene by the grave, the girl split in two, Steve lying dead in a pool of gore. 'Maybe they...summoned her.'

'You mean a ritual?' suggested Grady.

'Yeah. Something like that. The cross was on fire.'

'Maybe that's what did it? They, y'know, desecrated her grave. Would that work?'

'I don't really know the ins and outs of resurrection, Grady.'

He didn't respond, and she apologised.

She considered slowing the van again, but they were nearing the bottom of the mountain, and would need all the momentum they could get once they hit the main road. The overgrown scenic parking area shot by, a picnic bench faintly visible against the night sky. She figured they had no more than a mile of dirt track left.

'What does she want?' said Grady.

Beth felt sick. She knew the answer. They both did.

Maggie had told them.

'She wants her baby,' she said.

'Shit,' said Grady. He was quiet a moment, then said, 'Let's go to the town hall. We'll be safe, the whole town is there.'

'Not *everybody*,' said Beth. 'Not Alice.' She paused. 'And not Eric.'

Grady understood the implication.

'We don't know that's who she's come for. The hall is nearer. We need to get there first, then we can—'

'We need to warn Alice.'

'I *know*, but we don't have much choice. That thing is probably following us.'

'It doesn't matter,' said Beth. 'Pretty soon we're gonna run out of mountain.'

'So?'

'So then we slow down until we stop. It's only gravity keeping us going, remember? It's not gonna take us to the town hall. Hell, it's not even gonna get us into Auchenmullan.'

Grady looked at her fearfully. 'We're fucked, then. We're totally fucked.'

Beth cleared her mind, trying to think. 'We can run to the bowling alley. It's the nearest building, and it has a phone.'

Grady stared at her, but she kept her eyes on the road.

'Will Jack still be there?'

'I hope so,' she said, taking too long to answer.

Neither of them knew what to say to that. Jack *had* to be there. If not, then they were—

'Okay,' said Beth, casting the thought aside. 'So that's about half-a-mile along the main road. I'm gonna stop using the brake and try to build up as much speed as possible, see how far I can take us. At least we've got a head start.'

'But what if she's not been following the roads?'

'What do you mean?' This was not the time for stupid questions.

'I mean, what if she just went down in a straight line? She doesn't need to take the road.' His face was ashen. 'Jesus, she could be down there already.'

'In that case, shut up and keep your eyes open. It's nonstop all the way. And if Maggie Wall is waiting for us, I'm gonna mow that bitch down. When the van stops, get out and head for Jack's. We need to stick together. If Jack's gone home, we're all we've got.'

'He'll be there,' said Grady. The track dipped to the right, leading to the main road into town. Beth eased the wheel, steering them onto the tarmac, the velocity propelling them onwards. In the distance, she could see the lights of the bowling alley.

Please be there, Jack, she thought.

He had to be.

He simply *had* to be.

17

THEY HIT THE TARMAC AT FULL SPEED.

Beth chanced a nervous glance in the wing mirror. Nothing but darkness.

Good.

Maybe Maggie was still up there, on the mountain. Hell, maybe she couldn't leave it?

The van rolled on. There was a slight, almost imperceptible downward slope that kept them going further, but it wouldn't last. Sure enough, the van slowed.

'Should we get out?' said Grady.

Beth shook her head. 'Not until it's slower than our jogging pace.'

Soon then, she thought. *Very soon.*

Loose gravel crunched under the tyres, as the old WELCOME TO AUCHENMULLAN, PLEASE DRIVE CAREFULLY sign rolled past.

She looked at Grady. 'You ready?'

'Don't have much choice,' he said.

She hooked her fingers in the door release, the metal cool against her skin.

'This can't be real,' said Grady in a choked voice. He sounded like he was losing it, and she couldn't afford to let that happen. He had been there for her when she got back to the van. Now she needed to return the favour.

'Grady, listen to me. Maggie Wall is coming for us. I don't know how, and I don't really know why, but in two seconds we're getting out of this van and running for our fucking lives. Do you understand me?'

'Yeah,' he said unconvincingly.

'Grady, I can't do this alone. I'm scared too.'

It was almost time. She grabbed his arm.

'Are you ready?'

He nodded, his fists clenching.

'Let's do it.'

It was as good as she was gonna get for now.

Beth pulled the handle, and the door opened, the force of the wind pushing against it. She jumped, her feet landing perfectly, but the angle was all wrong. She lost her balance and fell, rolling onto her back. The van kept going, trundling past her. Grady ran to her, took her hand, and hauled her up.

'You okay?'

Beth tested her weight, moving from one foot to the other. She was fine.

Thank fuck for that.

She didn't want to be one of those idiots in a horror film who're always twisting their ankles when they're running from the killer.

With no one to steer the van, it swerved to the side, coming to rest at the foot of an embankment. Together, they jogged past, and Beth realised she would never sit in Steve's dad's van again.

Goodbye, Greener Pastures, with your mirror ball and your stupid old radio and your weird sex-cushions.

Grady set the pace. 'Control your breathing,' he said. 'Three seconds in, three seconds out.'

Beth tried it. It reminded her of the one time she had accompanied Alice to her prenatal class. It was all about breathing exercises for during the birth, *three seconds in, three seconds out.* She remembered being so bored by it, feeling that Alice was slipping away from her.

God, she had been so selfish.

'You okay?' asked Grady.

She nodded, not wanting to speak, afraid of upsetting her rhythm. The backlit sign of the alley was visible through the early-evening gloom. Without realising it, she sped up at the sight, her feet pounding the road, each loose pebble stabbing through the soles of her running shoes.

The alley was close...it was *so close...*

A shriek echoed out across the valley, coming from all around them, from everywhere and nowhere all at once, a terrible sound that chilled Beth to her marrow. She looked back, expecting to see Maggie, blood-soaked arms outstretched, grasping and clawing.

There was nothing there.

The wind sighed through the sagging branches of the trees, carrying the last remnants of Maggie's cry. Had she seen them? Was she nearby?

'Almost there,' said Grady. 'Keep going.'

Glass shattered behind them. They turned, and there she was, Maggie Wall, Witch of Auchenmullan. She was far in the distance, standing by the van, one of its doors lying by her feet. Beth was surprised at how much ground they had covered. It felt like seconds since they had leapt from the moving vehicle.

Maggie turned, her long neck pivoting towards them, eyes gleaming wickedly in the moonlight.

'Run,' said Beth, and run they did, like Satan himself was on their tail. The bowling alley loomed before them, a lone red Fiat parked out front.

Jack's car.

He must be still there.

Beth tried to think where Jack lived, but she couldn't remember.

Does it fucking matter right now?

Her legs ached. Christ, when was the last time she had run anywhere? In Auchenmullan, there was nowhere to run *to*. It was a sleepy place for sleepy people. She hadn't run since high school, that was for sure. The only time her heart rate increased was when she was having sex with Grady, and she hadn't done *that* for months. Her lungs tightened, a deadly snake coiling around them. Soon it would sink its fangs into her heart. Still, at least she was finally putting her running shoes to good use.

'Not far now,' wheezed Grady, and Beth knew he must be feeling the same way. Maggie sprinted after them, her spindly legs closing the gap with alarming speed.

They reached the car park and headed for the entrance, the sensor-light illuminating the area with its obscene three-hundred watt glare. The metal shutter was down, the rusted CLOSED sign in place.

But Jack's car is there. He has to be inside.

They slammed into the shutter.

'Jack! Let us in! For god's sake, let us in!'

Beth looked back and saw her, for the first time really *saw* Maggie, as she emerged into the light in all her ragged glory.

She was tall and grey, her limbs rotted and hideously

extended. Her grinning head was perched atop an elongated neck that swayed meanderingly as she moved, like a mountain stream. And there, *there* was the gaping cavity in her belly, where once upon a time the men of the town had torn her open and removed her unborn baby. Despite her decayed form, blood still gushed from the wound, splattering on the ground in an endless, terrible waterfall.

'Jack! Jack, open up! Let us in!'

Tears blurred her vision. She felt like giving up, lying down and letting Maggie Wall rend her limb-from-limb. She wanted to lie there and scream, *I don't have your baby! Alice does! She's not here!*

No!

Not Alice. How could she even think that?

'You lot clear the fuck off,' came the grizzled, alcohol-drenched voice of Jack. *'Fuckin' jakey wee cunts.'*

It was Jack, alright. Beth had never been so happy to be called Alice's least-favourite word.

'Jack! Let us in! Please!'

'She's going to kill us,' shouted Grady.

'Yer all fucking high. Piss off.'

'Jack, please! Steve's dead!'

The door behind the shutter opened, the vague silhouette of Jack visible through the gaps in the metal. Beth checked the parking lot. Maggie was getting closer, the infernal dripping blood somehow audible over the sound of her screams and fists striking steel. Maggie swirled forwards like smoke, as if the wind itself was controlling her, a tornado of fevered dreams.

'Where's...my...baby?'

Suddenly Jack was on his knees, working the lock free with shaking fingers. 'My god...my god...' he kept saying.

'Hurry!'

She was in the lot now, closing in on them, unhurried, like she knew there was nowhere to hide.

She was right. Everything depended on Jack now.

'Where's...my...baby?'

God, that *voice*, like Satan gargling blood.

The lock came free.

'Help me,' grunted Jack, taking the bottom of the shutter and lifting. Grady dropped to his knees, shoving his hands beneath the creaking barrier. Jack grabbed an old bucket and stuck it under the metal, holding it in place.

'Hurry!' he cried.

A shadow reared up over them. Beth scrambled inside, Jack dragging her in by her parka. She rolled onto her back and looked below the shutter. She could see Grady's Nikes, and behind those the wicked bony legs of Maggie advancing on him. Grady flattened himself. Beth grabbed one of his hands, Jack the other, and together they pulled him through the gap.

That was when Jack — who had drunk more than a few whiskies — lost his footing.

His feet slipped out from under him and he fell, his right foot striking the bucket that held up the shutter. It skittered out from under the metal and the shutter dropped, slamming hard on Grady's trailing ankle. Grady roared in agony. Beth pulled harder, but his foot was trapped. Jack gripped the barrier and tried to yank it up, but he was winded from the fall. Grady's eyes widened.

'She's got me! Jesus, she's fucking got me!'

Maggie dragged Grady backwards, the sharp edge of the shutter slicing through his calf muscle. In one almighty movement, Grady slid back through the gap up to his knee. Jack and Beth took a hand each, pressing their feet against the wall to prevent Grady from vanishing any further.

A hand, thin and distended, appeared from beneath the shutter, groping across the floor, the long fingers tapping against the wood. Jack and Beth shared a look, and then Jack did the unthinkable.

He let go of Grady and ran, disappearing into the alley.

'Come back you bastard!' screamed Beth, as his scurrying footsteps trailed off. The shutter pressed down on Grady's leg.

'Help me,' he sobbed, an ever-widening pool of blood surrounding him. Something was emerging from the other side.

Maggie.

The top of her head protruded like a tumour, slowly revealing itself on the end of that maddening long neck. Her eyes found Beth.

Maggie smiled. Her head was shrivelled, the skin frayed and loose over the bulbous skull, hanging in strips. The dry flesh around her mouth cracked like plaster, flakes drifting delicately to the floor.

Beth stared helplessly at her. There was nothing she could do now. Jack had run, left her here...that coward...that *bastard!*

Maggie looked past her, and before Beth could follow her gaze, she heard the voice.

'Move!' shouted Jack.

Startled, Beth just stared at him. He stood before her holding a handgun.

'I said fucking *move!*'

Beth shifted out of the way as Jack took aim at Maggie's head.

Maggie craned her neck to see him. She smiled with yellowing, sharpened teeth, then struck, lashing her head towards Jack, her jaws opening wide.

He squeezed the trigger.

The bullet caught Maggie square in the mouth. Her front teeth shattered, rattling across the floor like miniature bowling pins, and the back of her skull erupted in a puff of silvery dust. Her head ricocheted off the shutter and withdrew with extraordinary speed.

'Get him in,' said Jack, raising the shutter, straining his muscles to hold it up. Beth heaved Grady through the gap as Jack released the metal barrier and it crashed to the floor with a metallic clang that reverberated throughout the darkened room.

The three of them remained motionless, Beth holding Grady's hand, Jack staring at the smoking barrel of his revolver.

And Maggie?

Well, she was outside.

For now.

18

Inside Auchenmullan Town Hall, Inspector Lawrence Carlisle stepped out from between the curtains on the small stage and strode to the podium. There was a microphone there, though it wasn't switched on. It didn't need to be, not when there were only forty-odd people within earshot. His booming voice, honed by thirty years of police work, was loud enough.

Okay, thirty years was pushing it. He had been on the force for that long, but the last few years had felt more like retirement. Being Chief of Police in a town like Auchenmullan meant his most important task was chairing the monthly town meeting.

It had only been three weeks since the last one, and what a typically dreary affair that had been. He looked down at his notepad, reading the scribbled minutes from the previous meeting while he waited for the attendees to settle themselves down. Most of the page was covered in doodles. There were a couple of notes about a particularly sharp bend on the road out of town — Mark Fargen demanded the imposition of a slower speed limit, which was out of

Carlisle's jurisdiction — and Margaret Campbell wanted the shoe tree to be labelled as an official town monument.

Stupid bitch, he had scribbled on his pad.

Clive Moonie had asked about the lack of internet. Carlisle smiled as he recalled the exchange.

'*Why's that, Clive? You don't want to buy your porn the old fashioned way?*' he had said, and the crowd had snickered. Clive maintained it was something about improving the tourist trade, a way to bring some money into the town, but Carlisle thought that was the last thing they needed. It was best to just let the whole place rot. Once they were gone, maybe Auchenmullan would curl up in its grave and just fucking *die*.

'Everybody present?' he asked, looking up from his notes. The motley crew before him nodded, murmuring amongst themselves, sipping from the complimentary apple juice he had provided on entry.

No expense spared, he thought.

'Where's Elaine?' said someone.

Carlisle looked back to his notes. Right now, Elaine Burman was lying in her bed with bullet holes in her face and stomach. There had been no time to deal with her remains. That would come later, hopefully tomorrow, when the survival of the citizens was no longer at stake.

'Elaine won't be along tonight,' he said.

Or ever again.

He cleared his throat. 'I imagine you all know why we're gathered here one week earlier than planned.'

Another murmur passed through the crowd. Margaret Campbell stood.

'Are we here to discuss the shoe tree?'

Jesus wept.

'No, Margaret, not tonight.'

'I think we should. People could come from all over the world to see the shoe tree, and hang their own shoes on it. Honestly, it'll be the talk of country! In no time, we'll have the most wonderful shoe tree in Scotland.'

Carlisle had never met a woman who could talk for so long about a pair of trainers hanging from a fucking tree.

'Fine, I'll add that to my notes,' said Carlisle, scribbling *shove that tree up your arse* on his notepad.

'Don't forget, It's Shoe Tree with a capital S and a capital T,' said Margaret.

Carlisle smiled and amended his notes to *Shove that Tree up your arse*.

He motioned for her to sit, wanting nothing more than to wring her neck. Did she not realise what was happening out there? Time was running out.

'If no one has anything else to add,' he said, trying to maintain his carefully cultivated authority, 'perhaps we should talk about the return of Maggie Wall?'

Silence descended. He watched as they fidgeted in their seats, no one quite sure what to say.

Peter Lamb got to his feet, staring at Carlisle over the rim of his expensive glasses. 'I thought we agreed never to speak that name,' he said, looking around for support.

Carlisle snorted. 'Aye, we agreed. We all did, after the last time. And yet here we are.'

'This is different,' said Lamb. 'We've been cautious. Where's your proof?'

'Don't tell me you haven't felt it,' said Carlisle. 'It's in the air. Ever since the birth of the Burman boy, we've all noticed it. A change in the atmosphere, like the start of a new season.'

'You're talking shite,' shouted Evelyn Ronald, one of the town's more outspoken residents.

'Am I, Evelyn? Tell that to your fucking dog, who's been barking every night for the last few weeks.'

Evelyn flinched. 'It's the rabbits,' she said quietly, sitting back down. 'He's barking at the rabbits.'

'Aye, you tell yourself that.' He shook his head and addressed the crowd. 'Tell yourself whatever lets you sleep at night. But make no mistake, we all know it's happening again.'

'But we were *careful*,' said Lamb. 'The Burman girl gave birth in Inverness, not here.'

'Aye,' said Colin Foster, widow of two years, father to countless children across the region. 'But do we know where it was conceived? I've heard the Burman lassie's a right wee shagger.'

'They all are,' said June Trotter. 'All the young ones nowadays. S-e-x this, s-e-x that. It's disgusting.'

'Regardless,' said Carlisle, trying to bring some order to the discussion, 'Maggie *has* returned.'

'Nonsense,' shouted an unidentified voice in the crowd.

Carlisle pounded his fist off the podium. 'I saw a light in her cottage this very night! Now you can deny it all you like, but it doesn't change the fact that Maggie Wall is coming back, and she will not stop until she has that baby!' He took a breath. 'You were all here last time. You remember it. We stopped her.'

'By killing a child!' roared Peter Lamb, getting back to his feet.

'By performing the ritual,' corrected Carlisle, his temperature rising. 'The way it's been done for centuries, by our fathers, and their fathers before them. What will it take to make you believe? We have to act now, before she returns.

It could be tomorrow.' He paused for dramatic effect. 'It could be tonight.'

Agreement rippled through the crowd.

'Don't you hear yourselves?' said Lamb. 'You would murder an innocent on the whims of this charlatan?'

'Shut up, you speccy cunt,' someone shouted.

'Aye, fuck off if you don't like it.'

Lamb looked imploringly at the crowd, but no one wanted to hear him. 'It's murder,' he said. 'If we kill another child, we're no better than that *thing* that lives on the mountain.'

'Better the baby than me,' said Jordy McAleece. 'I retire in two years.'

'It's one life to save us all,' said Henry Waters.

Carlisle smiled thinly. 'You've been outvoted, Peter.'

Lamb shook his head in dismay. 'The Lord will judge you,' he said.

'All in due course, Peter,' said Carlisle. 'Now, I think you should leave. Looks like the meeting will have to continue without you.'

'My God,' he said. 'Is that why Elaine Burman isn't here? Have the killings already begun?'

'I said I think you should *leave*, Peter,' said Carlisle. 'And be careful out there. Locking your door won't help.'

'This town's blood is on *your* hands,' he said, pointing at Carlisle. He looked around, at the faces of his friends, his neighbours. 'It's on *all* of your hands.' He shuffled along the row of people. Someone tripped him and he fell to his knees. They laughed at him as he picked himself up and started towards the exit, holding his head high.

'One more thing, Peter,' said Carlisle.

The man stopped and turned to him, his hand resting on the door.

'What? Are you going to kill me too?'

'Not at all. Just a friendly remember that if you take this to the authorities, you're not so innocent yourself. You were present last time. You partook in the festivities. You may have washed the blood from your hands, but the stench of hypocrisy lingers a long, long time.'

'Then I'll see you all in hell,' said Lamb. He slid the enormous locking mechanism to one side, opened the door, and left.

There was a moment of silence.

'Anyone else have something to say?' said Carlisle. 'Speak now or hold your tongue.'

Annette Macleod raised her hand, and Carlisle nodded at her. She stood nervously. 'It's true what Peter said. We tried to avoid this. As is law, the bairn was born outside the town. So why would Maggie...I mean, why would *she* come back? We need to know if the child was conceived here. If so, that changes everything we thought we knew.'

'The child was conceived outwith the borders of the town,' said Carlisle. 'I confirmed that with the mother not long ago.'

'Who would believe a wench like her?' shouted Shirley Bannatyne. 'She should bloody well prove it.'

'I wouldn't have called this meeting if I wasn't sure,' said Carlisle. 'Most of you were here in eighty-five. You remember it. The carnage. The blood-letting. We had grown complacent, thought we knew better than the old ways. A lot of good men and women lost their lives that day. Who amongst you wants to be responsible for the same thing happening again?'

He let that sink in.

'Because let me tell you, there's a lot less of us than there was back then. If Maggie ventures down from her mountain...she won't spare a single one of us.'

He hadn't realised he had been shouting. The blank faces of the crowd looked back at him with glassy eyes. He stepped away from the podium.

'Listen, we're running out of time. I want to get this over with, so that I can go home and drink myself to sleep. Maybe, when I'm on my death bed, I'll have forgotten this ever happened, but I doubt it. We will *all* remember. This will haunt us to our graves, but it's too late to do anything about that now. We've done it before, and should the need arise, we'll do it again.'

'Let's get it over with,' shouted a faceless voice. 'Kill the little bastard.'

Carlisle nodded. 'Aye, that's the spirit,' he said half-heartedly. He took no pleasure in this, despite what that prick Peter Lamb seemed to think.

'Not yet!' shrieked Shirley. 'We need answers! What if that other slut, the Collins girl, gets—'

'That's my daughter you're talking about!' shouted Karen Collins, Beth's mother.

'Well, she's a wee toerag. We've all seen her underwear hanging on the washing line,' said Shirley. 'Dreadful skimpy things that leave nothing to the imagination. It wouldn't surprise me if she was canoodling with the Cooper lad right this instant!'

'Canoodling,' muttered Harry Cooper, Grady's father. 'Good on him if he is.'

'My daughter doesn't do that sort of thing,' shouted Beth's mum.

'*Silence!*' roared Carlisle. He ran his hands through his blond hair and slowly looked up at them. 'We don't have time for this. Karen, your daughter does wear some provocative clothing. Remember last year when I almost arrested her for swimming nude in Spectre Loch?'

'That was—'

'I'm not finished,' he snapped. 'We can discuss your daughter later. Shirley raises a valid point. We need to find out the details of the pregnancy so we can prevent this from happening again. And on that note, I have some good news for you.'

He walked to the curtains and took one of them in his meaty hand.

'You see, Peter Lamb was correct. I had to eliminate Elaine Burman when she refused to comply with the town laws. Unfortunately, there was a witness.'

He tore the curtains wide open. The crowd gasped, some in horror, some in what sounded like delight.

For there, clad in the traditional ceremonial white dress, was Alice Burman, her mouth gagged, her hands tied to the old cross that had fallen from the church roof in the big storm of 2007. Mascara tears rolled down her red cheeks. She tried to scream, but couldn't. Beside her, in a wicker basket, slept Eric Burman, her son. Carlisle looked out over the townspeople.

'If you have any questions for Miss Burman, this will be your last chance to ask her,' he said. 'For the ritual is about to begin.'

19

'HOW'S YOUR LEG?' SAID BETH.

Grady sat propped up on a chair by the wall, his damaged leg resting on the pool table.

'Hurts like hell,' he winced.

The shutter had gouged a huge chunk out of his calf. His trousers were torn up to the knee, a large flap of skin drooping. Beth watched it sway hypnotically. She took a soaked dish-cloth from the sink behind the bar, and carefully wiped away the blood, avoiding the exposed, tender flesh wherever possible. Was it salvageable? Or should she cut the flap off? The idea made her queasy, the thought of taking a pair of scissors, putting the loose flesh between the blades, and...*snip.*

She looked away, sickness bubbling within her.

It had gone quiet outside.

'What did you do?' said Jack quietly, sitting on the decrepit sofa, the gun resting across his lap.

'We didn't *do* anything,' said Beth, a little too sharply.

'You've gone and raised her, you've gone and raised Maggie Wall, may the devil rest her soul.'

'We didn't raise anybody. She just...woke up.'

'You've brought hell to this wee town. Aye, you've only gone and raised hell, you daft wee shites.'

Beth thought it best to say nothing. She worked up the courage to inspect Grady's leg again, trying to avoid looking at the dangling flap of flesh. Five bruises snaked their way around his calf, the skin cracked and peeling where Maggie had held him.

'Are there any other entrances?' said Beth.

Jack stared at the gun. 'Aye. There's the supply area. It's got an electric shutter, sealed up tight. That's it. Front and back, both secure.'

'You should have seen what she did to the van,' said Beth.

'Cars are designed to do that on impact,' he said, somewhat patronisingly. 'These shutters are solid. You felt the weight of them.'

She nodded and let him get back to his muttering.

So that was it — two entrances, both closed, and there were no windows. It was a health and safety nightmare, but she had to assume Maggie wouldn't be starting fires any time soon.

She hoped not, anyway.

The only way in that Beth could see was the skylight high above them. There was nothing they could do about that, except hope Maggie didn't climb onto the roof. And if she did?

Then we're royally fucked.

'What...are we going...to do?' said Grady, each word an effort.

'Call the police,' said Beth. 'And I don't mean Carlisle. Call out of town.'

'And tell them what?' laughed Jack. 'That a witch is trying to kill us?'

'Tell them whatever they want to hear. Whatever will bring them out here with guns and cars.'

Jack exhaled noisily and raised his head. 'It won't do any good. She'll destroy them. She won't stop, not until...'

'Until what?'

He stared at her, his eyes resigned and fearful. 'Until she gets your friend's baby. That's what she wants.'

'How do you know?'

Jack stood, calmly tucking the gun into his waistband, and headed over to the bar. He poured himself a pint of Black Isle IPA, then another. 'Come and sit with me,' he said. Grady's eyes were closed, and Beth checked his pulse. It seemed normal. She kissed him on the forehead and joined Jack at the bar. He slid the pint towards her and took a long drink of his own.

Then, when he was ready, he said, 'This isn't my first experience with Maggie Wall.'

Carlisle ripped the gag from Alice's mouth, and she choked, her lips white, her tongue dry. She gulped down lungfuls of air, as the crowd booed and jeered her, a crowd of people she knew and had grown up amongst.

Her eyes flitted across the furious faces. There were Beth's parents, Grady's, Steve's. There was Margaret Campbell, and Frank Hopper, and Clive Moonie, and... and...*everyone*. The entire town, people who had sold her groceries, babysat her, smiled at her in the street. Now they shouted as she stood helpless, tied to a cross like Jesus fucking Christ, her baby — her sweet, innocent baby — out of reach.

'Silence, please,' ordered Carlisle, and the crowd quietened, though not entirely. Mrs Hansen — Alice didn't know her first name, she had always been plain old Mrs Hansen to her — pointed an accusatory finger.

'Where was the baby conceived, you little tramp?' she shouted.

Alice tried to speak, but her throat had shrivelled. 'Water,' she croaked, glancing imploringly at Carlisle. Clive Moonie in the front row got to his feet and stormed up the stairs to the stage.

'I'll give you water,' he said, and spat in her face to cheers from the townspeople.

'Clive, please,' said Carlisle.

'What? She couldn't keep her filthy legs shut, so now we're all going to die?'

'Not if we complete the ritual!'

The phlegm dribbled down Alice's cheek. 'Why are you doing this?' she said quietly. Clive Moonie went back to his seat, as Carlisle took his plastic cup of water from the podium, and held it to Alice's lips.

'There, there,' he said, 'Just answer their questions and we can get on with matters. It'll all be over soon.'

'It's been going on for centuries,' said Jack, staring into the bottom of his glass. 'After what they did to Maggie, who can blame her?'

'What are you talking about?' said Beth.

Jack took a long drink, slammed his glass down, and belched. 'I'm talking about Maggie Wall. They took her baby, and no one knows what they did with it. That's what she's looking for. Her baby. Ever since her death, she's come down from the mountain to collect the newborns of Auchenmullan. Once she has them, she goes back...wherever she came from.'

'That's impossible,' said Beth. 'When I was growing up, there were hundreds of people living here. Almost a thousand at one point. Are you telling me there were never any births here?'

'Not in Auchenmullan, no. There's no hospital here, no doctors. As long as the wee ones are born outside the town, she doesn't seem to notice, as far as we could tell.'

Beth had too many questions. This was insane. 'And what if the child *was* born here? What then?'

'Then Maggie will not stop until she finds it. And if anyone gets in her way? She'll kill them too.'

Beth started to speak, but Jack held up a nicotine-stained finger. 'Wait, let me call the police, and I'll tell you the rest.' He left her there, wandering over to the pay phone and dialling. Beth sat in shock, her beer untouched. How could any of this be possible? It had to be a nightmare, a hallucination...and yet it wasn't. It was all too real. Thank fuck the phone lines were still working.

You're safe in here, but Alice isn't.

There was nothing she could do about that now, other than wait for the police to show up. Hell, she was already looking after Grady. There he was, dozing against the wall, his mutilated leg on ghastly display. He would be fine, though. The blood loss was bad, but it wouldn't kill him. They just had to wait. That was all it was now, a waiting game. And if Maggie was still outside, then all the better. It meant she wasn't running amok throughout the town. Her parents were still there, after all.

She felt awful. That was the first time she had thought of them since this nightmare had begun.

She picked up her pint glass and drank. The amber liquid went down easy. Jack was still on the phone, his voice raised. What if they didn't believe him?

They will. He's an adult, not a teenager. People believe adults, even when they're lying.

How many lies had she been fed, how many half-truths about Maggie Wall? If they had just been told about Maggie, that she was *real*, they would have been more careful.

Bollocks.

Imagine telling Steve not to do something and expecting him to follow orders.

Or yourself.

Poor Steve. There had been no time to mourn him, the big dumb jerk. She took another drink, her thoughts turning to Alice, and, inevitably, Eric. If anything were to happen to him, it would wreck Alice. It would destroy her.

'I won't let it,' said Beth, though what could she really do?

One thing needled at her. Jack said that Maggie only came after children born in Auchenmullan, but Eric had been born in Inverness...hadn't he?

'Tell the truth!' screamed a woman, her voice so shrill that Alice didn't recognise it.

'I am!' she said. 'I swear it's the truth! I had sex with Kevin once, and it was when we were skiing in Aviemore!'

She couldn't believe what was happening. Tied up in front of the town, while they barked questions about her sex life, demanding the most intimate details. It was every teenager's worst nightmare.

'She's only saying that to protect her baby,' cried someone.

'How do we even know the Johnson boy was the father? It could be anyone!' said another.

'He *is* the father! I haven't...' She started to sob. 'I haven't done it with anyone else.'

'What about with my son?' said a recognisable voice. It was Steve's mother.

Oh shit.

'You came home with him last year, around Christmas time. I heard you two in bed, you little slut. The walls in my house are *very* thin, you know.'

'We didn't have sex,' said Alice, her face red, eyes puffy from crying. She wriggled her wrists, trying to free herself.

And then what? Grab Eric and fight your way through the crowd?

If she had to, yes. Too fucking right she would.

'I heard you!' shrieked Steve's mum. 'I heard you corrupting my son!'

'He...he went down on me,' she said, aghast at the words leaving her mouth. Thank fuck her mum wasn't here to see this. 'That's what you heard. We kissed, we fooled around, and he—'

'Liar! Liar! She tricked my boy into fathering a child, and now she's brought doom to our town!' Steve's mother visibly shook, a trickle of blood running from her nose. She looked like she was having an aneurysm. Carlisle stepped forward.

'Alright, I think that'll do. Now do you believe me? Maggie Wall returns, and we've wasted half the night bickering like a bunch of fish-wives!'

'But the child wasn't born here,' said a lone voice of dissent.

'Then perhaps Maggie's changed the rules?' said Carlisle. 'All I know is, we're running out of time. Let's take a vote. All those in favour of the ritual, raise your hand.'

Alice watched, the life draining from her. They were voting the same way they chose the winner of the Prettiest Pig competition during the annual town fair.

'Please,' she screamed. 'Please, you *know* me! I've done nothing wrong! Do what you want to me, but leave my fucking baby alone!'

Carlisle didn't even need to count. Every hand in the room was raised.

He turned to Alice. On cue, Eric woke up and started crying.

'Not my baby...please...not my baby...'

Carlisle stood before her, the crowd baying for literal blood behind him. 'I'm sorry this had to happen,' he said. 'If your mother had just given up the baby, she might still be alive. And you would be safely at home, grieving over the unexpected loss of your first born. You'd be sad for a while. Distraught, even.' He patted her wet cheek with an open palm. 'But you'd get over it.'

'Don't hurt him,' she whispered. 'Please...don't hurt him.'

Carlisle smiled sadly.

'Aw sweetheart,' he said. 'It's too late.'

He blinked away a tear of his own.

'It's far too late for that.'

20

JACK PLACED THE PHONE BACK IN ITS CRADLE.

'That's the police on their way,' he said. 'Coming from Inverness, so they'll be about an hour. Had to tell them there's a fuckin' drug-crazed maniac on the loose. I think... oi, you listening?'

Beth wasn't.

Her eyes were fixed on the ten-inch black-and-white CCTV monitor nestled behind the bar. Jack's hand fell on her shoulder. She turned to look at his tired, sunken face, and wondered if she looked the same. He regarded her with something akin to drunken pity.

'Police are coming,' he said.

'Oh,' she said disinterestedly, turning back to the monitor. She felt Jack's eyes on her.

'You alright?' he whispered.

Beth nodded slowly. 'She's still out there,' she said, pointing at the frantic white-noise of the screen. 'See?'

Jack squinted. 'No,' he muttered, 'but then I shouldn't have bought my security system from Kenny Lachlan down the pub.'

'There,' said Beth, more insistently, and Jack spotted her. Maggie Wall.

She slithered around the building, hands skimming over the wall as if reading braille, then gazed at the camera, craning up towards it, her dire face filling the screen.

'Jesus...what's she doing?'

'She's trying to find a way in,' said Beth, repulsed by the spectacle.

'Then she's out of luck. There *is* no way in.'

She could feel Jack's breath on her neck, smell the booze-soaked waves coming off him. 'I hope you're right.'

'We're safe here. Just need to wait it out. The police'll arrive soon. Hopefully they won't send some rookie wee shite to his death.'

Maggie moved out of frame, and Jack leaned over and hit a switch, changing to a second angle.

'Where is she?' said Beth.

'I only have two cameras. There're a lot of blind spots. My god, I hoped I'd never see that face again.'

'Tell me what happened,' said Beth.

He sighed and poured himself another pint. Beth worried he was getting too drunk.

'I first saw her back in eighty-five,' he said. 'Some lassie was pregnant, didn't even realise it. I don't know how that's possible, but she was a bigger girl, y'know. Didn't really show. She gave birth at home, on Cherry Lane.' He stopped and took a long drink. When he put the glass down, it was empty. 'We weren't ready, we weren't prepared. By the time anyone knew about it, Maggie was on the High Street. Killed a dozen men and women before she reached Cherry Lane.' He lifted his glass again, realised there was nothing in it, and stared into the bottom.

'How did you stop her?'

'We tried. Christ knows we tried.'

She started to say something and stopped. She hadn't seen Jack like this before, his eyes wet with tears, as if the memory was causing him physical pain. He glanced at her, then looked at the monitor.

'I was one of the lucky ones. I survived. She left me with this, though.' He untucked his shirt, lifting it past his navel. Four deep red scars ran across his belly, six inches long. The surrounding skin was purple and diseased-looking. 'Never healed properly, but I can't complain, not after we arrived at Cherry Lane, and saw what she'd done to the mother. God, it was...'

He trailed off, staring into space.

Beth's arms broke out in gooseflesh. 'What about the baby?'

Jack shook his head, almost imperceptibly. 'We never found her. Maggie must have taken her...*home.*'

Movement on the monitor drew Beth's eyes away from Jack. It was Maggie again. She moved like falling snow, drifting and ethereal. A dark trail of blood followed her along the ground, pouring unendingly from the open cavity in her belly.

'That can't be the only time, though,' said Beth idly, transfixed by the ghoulish imagery onscreen.

'No, it's not. It happened again in eighty-nine, but that year we were ready. There's a way to stop her. That's what the meeting's about tonight.'

'So why aren't you there?'

He ran a hand through his grey hair. 'Because I'd rather die than witness that infernal ritual again. It's sick...depraved.'

'What do they do?'

'I told them I'd have no part of it, never again.'

She gripped his arm, squeezed it.

'*What do they do?*'

There was a sinking sensation in her stomach. She knew what he was going to say before he said it, but she needed to hear it out loud.

Jack cleared his throat.

'They sacrifice the baby.'

Her head swam. 'Alice...I have to warn Alice.' She elbowed past Jack, stumbling towards the telephone. He said nothing as Beth dialled Alice's house, her heart racing, listening to the dial tone. 'Pick up, pick up,' she chanted over and over, and then there was a click as someone answered.

'Alice, it's me, it's—'

'Hello, you've reached the home of Elaine and Alice Burman. We're not available right now, but if you'd like to—'

'Dammit,' shouted Beth. She slammed the phone into the cradle. 'Shit! Fuck!'

'What's happening?' said a weary voice. It was Grady.

'They're going to kill Alice's baby.' She pointed at Jack. 'You knew. All this time, and you *knew*. You let us sit here, thinking we're safe, but right now the whole town is—'

'What should I have done?' shouted Jack. 'Told you the legend of Maggie was true? You'd have fucking *laughed* at me, the lot of you. *Old Jack's going crazy*,' he said, waving his hands in the air. 'You kids don't listen. You just... never...listen.'

'What the fuck are you talking about?' said Grady. He looked like he'd been asleep for a hundred years. He shifted his foot onto the floor and grumbled in agony.

'Careful,' said Beth. She glared at Jack and went to Grady's side. His face was drained of colour, his skin clammy. 'Stay off your leg for now.'

'I forgot,' he said, tears forming in his eyes.

'Jack,' said Beth. 'Get me more painkillers.' She looked at Grady's savaged leg. 'And something to patch this up with. You got a fist aid kit?'

'There's some duct tape in the toolbox,' he said.

Grady's already pale face drained of any residual colour. 'Duct tape?'

'Just for now.' She tried to smile. 'It's better than nothing, right?'

He just looked at her with wide eyes.

She had to agree. It sounded horrendous, but anything was an improvement on watching that gross bit of skin flap about, or even — and the thought still disgusted her — cutting it off.

She took his hand. 'Jack phoned the police. They're on their way. We're gonna be okay.'

'Good,' said Grady. 'I'm really tired.'

'Me too.' She watched Jack amble past them. 'A little faster?' she snapped.

'Fuck off,' he said, and it made her smile.

For a moment, it almost felt like things were back to normal.

21

JACK RETURNED WITH AN ENORMOUS POWDERY PILL AND A roll of silver duct tape. Beth had already plied Grady with a double shot of whisky, and he lay partially dozing as she tore off an arm's length of the thick adhesive.

She heard a noise above her, and looked up in panic at the skylight, ready to see Maggie staring at her through the distorted, filthy window.

It was just rain, the heavy droplets bouncing off the skylight and running in rivers down the glass. That used to be Jack's cue to grab the big red buckets from the storeroom and lay them out below the cracks where the roof leaked, but not tonight. He sat alone behind the bar, watching the CCTV monitor and drinking.

Within minutes, the rainwater was trickling on the floor.

'Grady?' said Beth.

'Ugh?' he replied sleepily.

'This might hurt.'

'Ugh.'

She considered asking Jack for assistance, but decided

against it. If he had been drunk when they arrived, by now he was hammered.

Grady's foot rested on the pool table, the flap of skin hanging down. Beth, wishing for some gloves, took the piece between her fingers and slowly lifted it into place. The chunk of sinewy muscle was surprisingly heavy. It fit perfectly into the trench of Grady's wound, and she held it there, reaching for the strip of tape. She attached it to his shin bone, then carefully wrapped it around his calf. He shuddered and moaned, but didn't cry out.

He never could handle his whisky.

When she was finished, she stepped back and admired her handiwork. His leg was silver with tape, like an unfinished cyborg. She sat by him and stroked his hair. Part of her would always love him, she thought. It wasn't his fault they had ended up this way. Sometimes people outgrow each other. There's nothing to be done about it.

Shit happens.

'She's gone,' said Jack, from behind the bar.

'What?'

'I've been watching the cameras for the last fifteen minutes. There's no sign of her.' He looked at her hopefully. 'I think she's moved on.'

'We can't be sure of that.'

The words seemed to crush him. His shoulders sagged. 'We can't stay here forever.'

'We won't have to. The police are coming.'

'Aye. The police.' He got up and staggered drunkenly past them. His grey shirt was wet with sweat, dark patches around the neck and armpits.

'Where are you going?' said Beth.

'To take a shit,' he said, his words slurred.

She wished she hadn't asked.

He tripped over his own feet, bumping into the wall and mumbling, 'Fuck,' before he finally found the door to the men's room and made his way inside.

Moments later she could hear Jack's bowel movement splashing noisily into the toilet, and the occasional ripping fart.

'What's going on?' said Grady, eyes half-closed.

'Don't worry about it,' she said. 'It's just Jack.'

She supposed the sounds were normally masked by the jukebox, and had a sudden urge to play some songs. Music always made her feel better. It was a form of therapy.

But what if you attract Maggie?

So what? Maggie knew they were inside, and a little music was what they all needed right now. She dug a fifty pence coin from her pocket, popped it in the jukebox, and hammered in the numbers. She knew them by heart.

0-2-1

Michael Jackson, *Rock With You*. Her favourite song. Oh, she knew he was a weirdo, but that took nothing away from his music, and this song in particular. God, it was perfect. She nodded along, foot tapping in time, and glanced over at the barely conscious Grady, looking like The Terminator with his silly silver leg. Unable to help herself, she laughed.

She thought of Jack, sitting shitting in the other room, and of the undead witch waiting outside to tear them apart, and broke into hysterics. She danced, spinning in a circle, rainwater trickling from the crack in the skylight onto her head.

'What are you doing?' murmured Grady, but she was lost in the music. She remembered that stupid fucking fridge magnet her mum had bought in Inverness. *Dance like no one's watching,* it said. Beth had always hated it. It was almost as bad as *Live, laugh, love,* or — and this was undoubtedly the worst — *Keep calm and carry on.* She would rather walk into a room and see a giant neon swastika than one of those insipid sayings scrawled on the wall in a cursive font, and yet here she was — dancing like no one was watching, while outside, unimaginable death stalked her and everyone she knew.

Was this what madness was like? If so, it wasn't so bad. At least the music was good. She closed her eyes, clapped her hands and shook her bum, thinking of wild nights spent in The Vault nightclub with Grady and Alice and all their absent friends, balancing trays of drinks as she weaved through the dance floor, sneaking out to the smoking area for a crafty cigarette, Steve hitting on everyone...

Steve's dead now.

Her hands fell to her sides.

What are you doing?

She didn't know. For one glorious moment she had forgotten about everything, but now the horror crept up on her again. The song kept going, but Beth stopped dancing and stood under the leaking roof, staring at Grady. His eyes were shut, one leg twitching. What dreams tormented him? If they got out of this alive, she wondered if she would ever sleep again.

She wanted to dance some more, but the moment had passed, and she walked to the bar, feeling deflated. A drink, that was what she needed. Jack wouldn't mind. Hell, she'd likely be finished before he eventually emerged from the bathroom.

Two stone lighter, by the sounds of it.

She took a bottle from the fridge, her eyes flicking to the CCTV.

Jack was right. There was no trace of Maggie. The trail of her blood glistened in the glare of the lights, but she was—

Wait.

Beth gazed at the screen.

'What is that?' she asked no one.

It looked like a stick, but it was coming out of the wall. It disappeared inside. She rubbed her bleary, tired eyes. Was she seeing things? There was no way in, there was...

'Oh god,' she said.

The drainage pipes.

Maggie was in the *fucking pipes.*

Jack sat on the toilet, head in hands. He unleashed a hefty fart and tried to relax. So the police were coming...so what? By the time they arrived, it would be too late. Either Maggie would have decimated the entire town, or the baby would be dead. Carlisle would be livid that Jack had called the police, putting the town's hideous secret at risk, but he didn't care. He could handle Carlisle. The man was all blustering, impotent rage. He had no real authority here, not anymore. The only authority the town answered to had been dead for three-hundred years.

The water below him bubbled, spraying his arsehole like particularly bad splashback.

'Fucking plumbing,' he muttered. The pipes creaked and groaned through the walls. Bloody girls had probably been flushing their...*napkins*, or whatever they called them, and blocked the pipes again.

What a time for this to happen, he thought, trying to remember where he had last seen the plunger. A fucking witch outside waiting to kill him, and he was going to have to hand-pump shite out of the toilet. Life truly was magical. He chuckled to himself. At least they were safe in here. After

Maggie's last assault, he had bricked up the windows of the alley, and reinforced the steel shutters. The whole place was sealed up tight, nothing getting in, nothing getting out, the Alcatraz of third-rate bowling alleys. He felt sorry for the kids. They should have been told long ago, but would they have believed it? Kids are kids. They have to find things out for themselves.

The water bubbled again.

Christ, he couldn't concentrate. Taking a good shite was usually a highlight of his day, but that bubbling was driving him batty. He reached into the metal container affixed to the wall for some toilet paper. There was none.

'Fuck's sake,' he mumbled. There was some in storage. He'd have to get up and walk through there with a dirty—

He flinched.

'Ooooh,' he breathed, his buttocks clenching. 'What the fuck...?'

There was a sharp, stabbing pain in his arse. He tried to move, but it only made the sensation worse. 'Ow...ow...' he said. It was like something had *jumped* up in there. Putting his hands on the sides of the cubicle, he lifted himself a few inches, before something pulled him back down, hard, his back cracking off the cistern. He wanted to call for help, but he couldn't, not like this, sitting on the toilet with his cock out, his trousers and pants around his ankles. And what would he say? He's got a sore arse? Jack — who had refused to go for his prostate exam — would not put himself through the humiliation of Beth finding him like this. It was fine. He could sort himself out. What had he eaten for dinner? He—

'Jesus!' he shouted, his fists clenching, shaking, his nails digging into the flesh of his palms. 'Jesus fucking Christ on a bus!'

There was something else up there now, long and thin and pointed. He heard a tearing sound as his anus widened, ripping open, followed by the frantic splash of blood gushing into the toilet bowl.

He threw his head back in agony, his skull striking the flush button. Water poured into the bowl, filling it until it rose to the seat, immersing his arse and balls and spilling out over the sides, flooding the tiled floor. The water was thick and red.

Jack howled, unaware that just below him, somewhere round the U-bend, Maggie Wall was smiling.

22

'GRADY, WAKE UP!'

Beth shook him until his sleep-encrusted eyes flickered open and he stared at her in equal parts bafflement and fear.

'What's happening?'

'She's found a way in, come on, we have to get out of here.'

He tried to sit, dazed-looking. 'How? Where?'

'Can you stand?'

'I can try,' he said, hooking an arm around her shoulder. She lifted him, and he stood, unsteady, but up nonetheless.

Jack's painkillers must be pretty damn good, she thought, and briefly wondered what they were.

Shit.

Where was Jack? Still in the loo?

'Wait here,' she said. 'I'm going to get Jack.' She let go of Grady. He wobbled precariously for a second, then stood firm, taking a deep breath.

'Go,' he said, and she did, racing towards the bathroom.

'Fuuuuuuuck!'

The scream came from inside the men's room. Beth hurtled through the door and down the short corridor, passing the ladies' bathroom on the way. It wouldn't be her first visit to the men's toilets — she and Grady had passed the time in there on more than a few occasions — and she entered, facing the row of urinals. Opposite, in the corner, were the two stalls. The stench hit her hard, and she covered her nose.

'Jack, she's coming,' Beth shouted, her shoes squelching on the floor. 'She's in the pipes.'

The men's room was always disgusting, flooded in urine and stinking of bleach, but this was worse than normal. Her feet slipped out from under her, and she crashed onto the floor.

It was covered in blood, blood that poured in ichorous rivers from beneath the last stall, unending crimson waves of fresh gore soaking through her trousers.

'Help!' wailed Jack.

Beth got to her feet, unsure of what to do. The amount of blood that pooled around her shoes was inhuman. He couldn't still be alive, and yet he called to her, pleading. Gripping the sinks for balance, she shuffled towards the last stall. The door was wide open. She remembered Grady telling her that Jack never closed the cubicle door, prefer-ring to shit with it wide open. He had laughed when he told her of his surprise at finding Jack there, how he had looked up at Grady and simply said, *'Fuck off.'* Now she had a front-row seat all to herself.

He half-sat, half-stood, penis flapping between his legs, leaning forwards at an absurd angle. His hand was extended, desperately reaching out towards her. She recoiled, taking in the whole macabre scene. Blood flowed from his behind. There was something huge coming out of it. She gagged.

It's not coming out.

It's going in.

Whatever it was, it wriggled from within his stomach, five points scratching at the flesh from inside. The thing forced him back down onto the bowl, *into* it, his legs jutting out vertically. There was a gut-churning snap as his pelvis cracked, and then the claws inside him were higher, bursting through his jugular. Jack's neck bulged obscenely, his jaw dropping as four red fingers emerged from his mouth like a nightmarish spider.

Get the fuck out of here, her mind screamed.

As Jack's chest split open, revealing the grinning face of Maggie Wall, Beth scrambled from the bathroom, feet skidding in the blood, and burst out into the alley. From behind the closed door, she heard Maggie hiss, *'Where's...my...baby?'*

She looked for Grady, but he was nowhere to be seen.

'Beth, over here!'

She searched for the voice and there he was, leaning against a metal door, the words FIRE EXIT painted over with black emulsion.

'She's here,' said Beth. 'She's inside!'

'This way,' said Grady. He looked bad, like a nervous flier experiencing turbulence. Where was he taking her? The entrance was back the other direction. They'd have to unlock the door, raise the shutter, and by that point Maggie would have torn them to shreds. She could hear her footsteps, the bathroom door flying open and hitting the wall. One corridor was all that stood between Beth and certain death.

'Beth!' shouted Grady. 'Please!'

She ran to him, leaving dark red footprints on the

wooden floor, her blood-drenched clothes sticking to her skin.

'Through here,' said Grady, pushing the door open. Every word, every movement, was a Herculean effort. Whether from the blood loss, the shock, or Jack's pills, Grady was running on fumes. Beth took his hand and barrelled through the door into the waiting darkness. Grady followed, and with her last remaining shred of sense, Beth grabbed the door and slammed it shut.

She heard the thump of Maggie's feet drawing closer, and groped for the lock, finding it, sliding the bolt into place as the door shuddered under the impact of Maggie's reedy body.

Please hold, oh god please hold.

It did, but for how long?

The light came on and Beth screamed. Grady stood in the middle of the room holding the light-switch cord, favouring his undamaged leg. He released it, and it swung gently.

They were in the supply room. Cardboard boxes lined the walls, a large refrigerator humming in the corner. Boxes of crisps, fizzy drinks, and pallets of bottled beers sat on dusty shelves.

And there, in the centre of the room, stood salvation itself.

Jack's delivery van.

Though he mostly acted like a misanthropic asshole, Jack used to deliver his limited groceries to Auchenmullan's elderly residents. The rumour was that he didn't even accept payment for it. Lately, the van hadn't been seen around town. Most assumed he had sold it, but here it was, the white paintwork now a grubby shade of brown. Would it still drive?

Only one way to find out.

'Get in the van!' shouted Beth.

'The keys,' said Grady, unmoving.

'They'll be inside,' she snapped. She was sure they would be. This was *Jack* they were talking about, not James Bond.

She raced to the ancient control panel on the wall and hit the big red button. The shutter started to raise, juddering and clanking all the way. Grady had made it inside the van, which at least proved it wasn't locked. Maggie hit the door, turning it concave, several screws bursting from the hinges and rattling on the cold stone floor.

'No keys,' shouted Grady. 'I can't find the fucking keys!'

The shutter was halfway up and Beth ran towards the van, throwing herself in. Grady rummaged beneath the driver's seat, the glove box sitting open and empty.

'Hotwire it,' said Beth.

'I don't know how. Do you?'

'Of course not!'

'Well why would I?'

'I don't fucking know!'

The door flew off the hinges, soaring across the room and hitting the opposite wall. Beth, in full panic mode, wrenched both sun visors down. Out of one fell a spider, but the other was more successful. A set of keys jangled onto her lap, and she thrust them at Grady.

'Start the car!' she screamed, as she flung open the door and got back out of the van.

'Where are you going?'

Beth didn't answer. She hurtled over the bonnet and raced for the control panel again.

This has to work. It has to.

Maggie entered the room, her swooshing head peering

in like a cobra ready to strike. Her mouth opened and a gristly pink tongue ran across her remaining teeth.

'*Where's...my...baby?*' she said.

Grady started the van. It spluttered and died.

Please start, please start, please start, thought Beth, as she hammered her fist on the control panel and the automatic shutter jolted to a stop. She hit another button and it began to lower. Maggie came towards her, and Beth ran for the van, diving across the front and scrambling into the passenger seat once more.

The shutter was getting lower, the gap closing.

Grady cranked the key, and the engine bellowed like a wounded animal, the exhaust expelling thick, black smoke.

'Go!' screamed Beth, and Grady floored the pedal with his good leg, the van shooting forwards. The shutter scraped off the roof of the vehicle with a screeching sound, sparks cascading over the back window, and then they were out, free, the vehicle skidding on mud and heading for the gate.

They hit it going over thirty. The small padlock was useless against the impact, the gate smashing open. Beth checked the rearview mirror, catching a last glimpse of Maggie's legs as the shutter closed, locking her in. The barrier rattled as Maggie pounded against it, but it was too little, too late.

They had escaped.

They were *free*.

'We made it,' said Beth, sobs wracking her body. 'We fucking *made* it.'

23

ALICE KNEW SHE WAS GOING TO DIE.

What she had established, from their bizarre ramblings and increasingly insane questions, was that she and Eric were going to be murdered to appease the ghost of Maggie Wall.

Okay, not murdered. They were to be *sacrificed*.

What the fuck?

It would be laughable if they weren't deadly serious. Nothing she said could change their minds. They believed that Maggie Wall was alive, and would kill them unless they sacrificed Eric. She was just collateral damage, like her mother. The entire Burman clan, three generations, wiped out in one day, and all because of a goddam *ghost*. They were mental, the lot of them. Fucking mental!

She watched, her limbs aching, as they quietly cleared away the chairs, stacking them neatly against the walls. The ugly white dress itched her neck, and she badly wanted to scratch it.

She looked down at Eric, lying in his basket, his eyes open and staring at the ceiling. He reached a chubby hand towards his face, probing at his mouth, and Alice's heart broke in two. The love she felt for him, the need to protect him, overrode everything else, and she resumed her efforts to escape. What was that shit she had read about, of mothers finding superhuman strength and lifting cars off their children? Why couldn't she find *those* hidden reserves? Was she not a good enough mother?

The last of the chairs were slotted together, and several men gathered at a store cupboard. They entered one at a time, carrying out yoga mats and laying them down. What were they up to now? She had expected candles and pentagrams, not a fucking pilates class.

Carlisle stood by the podium like a minister preaching to his flock, directing their every move.

'Put that down there. No, next to the blue one. Make sure the door's locked. Paul, check the windows, and you two draw the curtains. Chop, chop, people, we need to get this done. You know the ritual takes time.'

This ritual he spoke of...what did it involve? Would they be tortured? She had seen this kind of bullshit in films, satanic rituals with hooded cultists chanting around a fire. It was always a woman being sacrificed, and they always made sure to rip her clothes off first. Were those films accurate? Was that how this would go down? She hoped that, if nothing else, they killed her first. That way, she would die knowing Eric still had a chance.

She watched as one of the older men anxiously tugged on Carlisle's shirt sleeve.

'What is it?' Carlisle snapped irritably.

'Listen, Larry,' said the man, an apologetic note in his voice. 'I'm afraid I'm getting too old for this.'

'Nonsense. You must participate.'

There was a buzz about the room now, an anticipation. The atmosphere was charged with a chilling electricity.

'It's just,' continued the man, keeping his voice low, 'the old equipment isn't quite what it used to be. What if I just sat this one out and watched?'

Carlisle turned to him, disgusted. 'Stop what you're doing,' he shouted. The old man's face turned scarlet.

'Aw, Larry,' he said.

Carlisle addressed the crowd. 'Listen up. You know how this is done. It's not our first time, and if we're lucky, it'll be the last. But we do it like we always have. The ritual has never changed, and we're not about to start now. You were all given a glass of apple juice on entry. That juice contained a stimulant.'

There was a low murmur amongst the crowd. Alice was dumbfounded. A stimulant? What was he on about?

'Oh quiet down,' bellowed Carlisle, 'and don't act so surprised. We're all getting on a bit, so I've tried to make this as easy as possible. We've got the mats, you've all taken the stimulant. I've even made a CD for the occasion.'

Alice could have sworn she was dreaming. Every word out of Carlisle's mouth was more deranged than the last. Stimulants? A mix CD? It sounded like they were teenagers on a weekend trip to Magaluf.

'What's happening?' she cried. 'What's going on?'

She made eye contact with Beth's mum, and the woman looked away. Beth's father didn't, though. He stared at her, his hand down the front of his trousers, moving rhyth-mically...

'Oh god, oh god,' she said.

Carlisle lifted a Tesco bag-for-life from beside the podium and removed two items. One was a shiny compact disc that caught the lights, momentarily blinding Alice. The other was a knife, the blade long, the handle intricately carved.

The murder weapon.

The sight of it sent Alice careening into a full-blown panic attack. She kicked, she thrashed, but still she could not wrestle free of her bonds. 'Leave him alone! Leave my son alone! I'll kill you all!'

Carlisle ignored her. He laid the knife by Eric's basket and took the CD over to the chunky black stereo system.

'Clive, dim the lights please,' he commanded, hitting a button on the stereo. The disc tray whirred out, and he placed the CD on it.

People began undressing, arthritic fingers fumbling with buttons, underwear lowered to reveal greying pubic regions.

'What the fuck are you doing?' screamed Alice.

Carlisle pressed the tray into the stereo, and seconds later the plaintive sound of an acoustic guitar echoed out over the muddy speaker system of the town hall. She vaguely recognised the tune from her childhood, the fingers delicately plucking a melody, soon joined in by a piano.

It wasn't…

It couldn't be…

It was *You're Beautiful* by James Blunt.

Alice looked to the crowd, but most of them were already naked.

Oh no no no no no no no no no…

Carlisle let his shirt flutter from the stage, standing topless before them. He fiddled with his jeans, and then they slid down to his ankles. He wore no underpants, his sagging buttocks on display. As James Blunt started to tell the world how precious his life is, and some bollocks about an angel, Carlisle spread his arms wide and spoke four words.

'Let the ritual begin.'

~

The van sped through the empty, silent streets of Auchenmullan.

The town had never felt so...dead. Beth watched the lights of the bowling alley recede into the murky darkness of the rearview mirror, and then they were gone forever. She tried not to think of Jack's gruesome demise, her mind instead turning to the horror they had trapped in the supply room. She swore she could still hear Maggie's lamentable shrieks over the monotonous roar of the engine. A shiver passed through her, and she felt cold all over. Her hand shook, and she couldn't stop it.

Was she in shock? Were the events of the last few hours — god, is that all it was — finally catching up with her? She had tried to be strong, for Grady, for her, but the reservoir she drew on was running dry.

She put her hands under her arse, but she could still feel the tremors in them. Somehow, breathing no longer came easy to her, a forgotten skill she had to relearn.

Beside her, Grady said nothing. It was too quiet. She wanted to shout, to scream, to release the tension that coiled inside her, tight and deadly.

'You okay?' she said, her voice little more than a whisper.

'Drowsy,' said Grady. 'What did you give me?'

'One of Jack's pills.'

Grady nodded. He blinked, his eyes staying closed too long for Beth's liking.

'Want me to drive?'

He shook his head. 'We're almost there.'

They passed his parents' house, the lights off, no one home.

Well, obviously! They're at the town meeting. On tonight's agenda — the Christmas jumble sale, how to improve tourism, and ritual sacrifice.

Were her own parents there? They had to be, but the idea was too unbearable to comprehend.

'You think it'll hold her?' she said.

'What'll hold who?' said Grady, his hands locked on the wheel.

'Maggie. You think she can get out?'

'Yeah,' he said.

'How's your leg?'

'Sore.'

His monosyllabic answers concerned her. It wasn't like him. The idiot usually never shut up, unless he was playing FIFA, in which case he spoke only in violent, despairing profanity. She needed to keep his mind active.

'Sure you don't want me to drive?'

'No.'

'But your leg?'

'It's just the one.' His face was drowsy and slack. 'As long as we don't need to brake in a hurry, we'll be fine.'

'Famous last words,' said Beth, and Grady pressed down on the accelerator to demonstrate. The van sped up.

Not long now.

'There's no one out there,' said Beth quietly. 'It's just us.'

'Everyone's at the meeting,' said Grady, and he was right, but it wasn't what Beth had meant. It really felt like the end of the world, and they were the last two survivors. They lapsed into silence as Grady navigated the streets, flagrantly ignoring the 20mph signs. Beth rested her head against the cool glass of the window.

'I'm scared,' she said.

'I know,' said Grady, the words leaving his dry, white lips with difficulty. 'So am I. But we're almost at the town hall. Our parents are there. They'll know what to do.'

It was a strange thing to say. Childlike, even. Did he not know what they were planning on doing to Alice's baby tonight? Had he been asleep when Jack told her? She couldn't remember. Everything was happening too fast.

'We need to pick up Alice,' she said. 'We need to get her and Eric far away from here.'

'Eric...' said Grady. 'I don't know an Eric.' He turned to her, his eyes wide and frightened. 'Do I?'

'Alice's baby,' she said. 'You...you remember she had a baby, right?'

'Oh, yeah. Sure I do,' he said.

Grady had never been a good liar.

'I think I should drive,' said Beth.

'I can do it. We're almost at the hall.'

'We're not going to the hall, Grady.' She spoke carefully. 'We're going to get Alice.'

He looked confused, disoriented. What the fuck was in those pills she had given him?

'Alice,' he said. 'She's our friend.'

'That's right.' She started to cry. 'That's right.'

Far above them, the already black skies darkened further, monstrous clouds threatening another torrential downpour, or even the promised snow. They careened round a corner, the van briefly mounting the pavement with a sharp bump. Beth's head smacked off the window, and she hardly noticed.

'Why are you crying?' said Grady.

She didn't answer.

The streets raced by outside, the abandoned houses blurring together.

'Slow down,' she said.

'But we're almost there.'

'We have to get there in once piece. We have to...*car!*'

Grady grinned sleepily. 'We have to car?'

'Grady watch out there's a fucking—'

He turned back just in time for the headlights of the Fiat to blind him. Panicking, he threw his hands up in front of his face, as Beth leaned over and grabbed the steering wheel, yanking it towards her, the van skidding.

She was too late.

The Fiat had also tried to move out of the way, and the two vehicles smashed into each other, their van — which had been going three times the speed of the small car — ploughing through the front of the Fiat and demolishing the engine.

'Brake!' screamed Beth, and Grady slammed his foot down as hard as he could, but his leg was weak. The van kept moving, leaving the road and bursting through a hedge, heading straight for an oak tree. It collided with the thick trunk, curling around it like an unwanted hug.

The impact threw Beth into her seatbelt, her neck whipping violently forwards.

There was a rustling noise high above her, in the tree. Something moving, brushing the branches aside.

As her eyes closed, a single pair of mouldy running shoes — which had hung from a branch near the top of the shoe tree for over a decade — thumped onto the bonnet, and then all was silent once more.

24

DRIP, DRIP.

Beth opened her eyes. Where was she? There was a tree in front of her.

That's a funny place to put a tree, she thought.

Her focus adjusted to the pair of trainers tied together by their laces that rested on the crumpled bonnet, framed by the broken windscreen. Smoke rose from the engine, only to be carried away by the wind.

Dazed, she sat for a moment, then tried to move her head, a tight pain needling at her neck. With shaking hands, she unbuckled her seat belt. Grady lay still, eyes closed, his chin resting on his chest.

'Grady,' croaked Beth.

Drip drip.

What was that noise? Blood?

She shook him.

'Uhhhh,' said Grady. It wasn't much, but it was better than nothing.

'Hey,' she breathed. 'Can you hear me?'

Grady nodded, his breath steaming in front of him.

Flakes of snow swirled in through the broken windshield, resting on the dashboard and melting away.

'It's snowing,' she said.

Grady's eyes flickered open. 'Where are we?'

'The shoe tree,' said Beth, glancing around at the smoking remains of the Fiat, and wincing at the pain that jabbed at her neck. 'We hit a car.'

'How long have we been here?'

'Not long,' she said. 'I don't think.'

How long *had* it been since they crashed? Seconds? Minutes?

'I'm gonna go check on the driver,' she said. She didn't want to. She wasn't even sure she had the strength. But he might still be alive, and she had to try.

'Maggie could be out there,' said Grady. Beth nodded. She knew that. What did Grady want her to do? Just wait in the van with him until Maggie arrived?

Drip drip.

She found the latch and pulled, half-expecting the door to be stuck. It opened easily, and she staggered around the van, resting against it with every step. Her body was weary, broken, a particularly nasty pain stabbing at her ribs. She imagined the long line of bruises down her chest and stomach from the seatbelt.

At least you're still alive.

The Fiat sat in the middle of the road. It had been totalled. The front of the vehicle was gone, seared off as if by a guillotine, and there were black marks on the tarmac from where it had skidded. There was something wet underfoot, and she realised Jack's old supply van was haemorrhaging petrol. Would it blow? There was no fire, no sparks. Safe, surely?

Someone sat in the Fiat, their head resting on the

steering wheel, and Beth noticed for the first time the sound of the horn blaring.

'Stop, she'll hear you,' said Beth, though she said it to no one. She reached the car and looked inside. It was a man. Was he dead? She leaned through the glassless window, putting her hand on his sticky forehead, and moved him back into the seat. The horn stopped abruptly, the new silence creating a ghostly emptiness.

It was Peter Lamb. He used to run a hiking supplies shop, and now taught PE at a school that was a two-hour commute.

Not anymore.

Now he was dead, and *they* had killed him.

'No,' she said, blinking away fresh tears. How much could one person cry?

Peter Lamb's nose looked like a burst tomato, his face an explosion of crimson. His front teeth were embedded in his lower lip right up to the gums, and shards of broken glass pierced his skin.

'I'm sorry,' said Beth, and when the dead man's eyes opened and looked at her, she could do nothing but scream. His lips parted, the teeth slipping free with a gruesome sucking noise, blood spilling over his chin.

'He was going too fast,' said Lamb, though it came out like '*ee wa gowah oo thas.*'

'I'm sorry.'

She didn't know what else to say. She had to help this man, and then Grady, and watch for a witch, and warn the adults, and pick up Alice and her son, and...and...

It was too much for one soul to bear, and she broke down. She couldn't do this alone.

Lamb placed a gnarled, broken hand on her arm, and gave her a grotesque parody of a comforting smile. She looked at the damage they had wrought across his face, and turned away. Through the lightly falling snow, she saw the street sign.

Mountainview Road.

They were only a couple of streets away from the town hall, from people...adults...

Murderers.

Then a dark voice in her head spoke.

Just wait until they've killed the baby. Go somewhere safe, hide, and all this will be over soon.

The thought horrified her. The idea was so vile, so abhorrent...and yet worst of all, she recognised the truth in it.

She looked over at the van, nestled snugly into the small area of parkland off Mountainview Road, wrapped around the shoe tree. Grady was still in the driver's seat. The airbag suddenly deployed, smacking him in the face, then quickly deflated. Grady didn't stir. It was not a good sign.

Overhead, a streetlight jittered nervously.

'Can you walk?' she said to Lamb.

He didn't answer. He just sat there, staring ahead. *'Aa-ee,'* he said.

'What? I don't understand.' The snow continued to fall. Soon the road would be a white blanket, and it would stay that way for the next four or five months. Jack would dig the sledges out from storage and hire them out, and she and Grady would go skiing on the Cairngorm mountains, and—

'Aa-eh,' said Peter, and now she knew exactly what he was trying to say. She followed his gaze down the street, knowing full-well what she would find there, waiting for her.

Maggie Wall.

Backlit by the strobing streetlamp, she resembled a tall sapling undulating in the wind, her restless head dipping and swooning through the night air. She had gone from a sickly white-grey colour to dark red, Jack's blood covering her body, flakes of skin caught on the spikes of her branch-like arms, stringy intestines dragged along behind her. Lamb didn't seem surprised to see her, and why would he be? They all knew about it. They all *knew*.

Beth backed away from the Fiat.

'I have to go,' she said, and Lamb nodded, turning his kindly eyes back to Maggie. He understood.

She couldn't save them both.

'Go,' he said, and she hobbled across the road to the van. Grady's door was open, one leg dangling onto the grass. She ran to him, her desperate hands fumbling with the buckle of his seatbelt. She put his arm over her shoulder and helped him out, looking back at Maggie bearing down on them, almost level with the Fiat. Peter Lamb was lumbering out of the car, clinging onto the door for dear life.

'Maggie!' he shouted, wiping a trail of blood from his chin.

Beth wanted to watch, but she had to get Grady to safety. *Leave him. Save yourself.*

That voice again...why couldn't it just fuck off?

Maggie stood before Peter, smiling that devilish, hypnotic smile.

'*Where's...my...baby?*' she said, and Beth's blood ran cold.

'Your baby's gone, Maggie,' slurred Lamb, doing his best to enunciate through shattered teeth and punctured lips.

Maggie tilted her head from side to side, grinning at him.

'Lift the curse, Maggie,' said Peter. 'You've destroyed this town. It's finished. Look around...there's nothing left! You've had your revenge. Please, just let the children live.'

As Beth helped Grady towards the town hall, moving impossibly slowly, she glanced back at Peter and Maggie.

They faced each other, Maggie towering over him. Peter rummaged in his pocket and pulled out a cigarette, stuffed it in his mouth.

Maggie watched him, blood flowing from the black pit in her body, where once upon a time a group of men had cut her open and forcibly removed her unborn child.

Was she listening? Did she understand?

Peter fumbled for his lighter and lit up, drawing in the smoke, welcoming the blessed hit of nicotine.

'Go home, Maggie,' he said, and then her claws were out, rending and tearing, peeling back flesh, exposing muscle and gleaming white bone. Lamb went limp and the lighter dropped from his hand, the flame catching on the petrol beneath his feet.

'Let the children live,' he said, as his world exploded in a cavalcade of flame, obliterating Peter Lamb and Maggie Wall where they stood.

25

Beth and Grady felt the heat on their backs, the shockwave sending them crashing to the road as the blast lit up the street like daylight. The flames spat along the ground, following the petrol trail to Jack's van.

'Keep going,' said Beth, her arm around Grady, helping him to his feet.

She chanced one last look back, and witnessed the blazing whirlwind of Maggie Wall pirouetting in fury like a literal living hell.

The van erupted next, knocking Maggie off her feet and sending her flying into the flaming debris of the Fiat. Peter Lamb's smouldering, blackened limbs were scattered across the road, and Beth looked away, nausea wrapping its dark tendrils around her frantically pounding heart.

They left Mountainview Road and carried on, coasting on nothing but the adrenaline that soared through their veins. The town hall was close. They could reach it.

Maggie's diseased wails reached a fevered maelstrom of insanity. Was she following? She would, but Beth figured Maggie had more important things to worry about right now. Perhaps the fire would kill her? Was that possible? Could they be that lucky?

She doubted it.

As they ran, she wondered what Peter Lamb had been doing driving the roads at this time of the evening. Shouldn't he have been at the meeting?

The sacrifice, you mean.

'Look,' mumbled Grady, and Beth saw the town hall ahead of them, the shutters closed.

'Why's it so dark?' she panted, her feet aching. Maggie's wailing had subsided, and when Beth checked, she was nowhere to be seen.

Please...let her be dead.

There were six or seven vehicles in the car park, including Beth's parents' silver Nissan. The sight of it made her heart quicken. All she wanted was her mum. The idea shamed her. She was a grown woman, but right now the most important thing was to hug her mum, to see her, to know she was still alive. She wanted to prove Jack wrong. Her parents wouldn't sacrifice a child to appease some grotesque, ancient evil. They were normal, boring people, like everyone else in Auchenmullan. They got up and went to work after a sensible breakfast, then came home and watched the telly and discussed politics. They weren't murderers...they weren't *savages*.

The moonlight shadows of the town hall stretched across the road, beckoning them.

'We're almost there,' cried Beth, Grady flopping in her arms.

The entrance was near. She looked around, but still there was no trace of Maggie.

They approached the town hall as Maggie Wall's blood-curdling wail split the night asunder, and Beth knew they were almost out of time. She left Grady sitting by the steps, and ran into the door at full speed, which was one hell of a way to find out it was locked.

'Fuck,' she shouted, her shoulder throbbing from the jarring collision. Since when did they start locking the town hall?

Probably when they started murdering babies.

She thumped her fists off the door until they stung, tears rolling down her cheeks in unending waves.

'Help! Let us in!' she screamed. There was no answer, and fear clouded her mind. 'It's Beth Collins! Open up!'

'Go away,' came the muffled response. Beth couldn't place the voice. She heard more people talking in urgent, frightened whispers, and stopped pounding on the door, laying her hands against it, pressing her face to the cold wood, the snow drifting around her.

'Mum?' she said. 'Are you in there?'

There was a subtle murmuring. What the fuck were they doing? She glanced round to see Grady climbing the steps, a pleading, haunted look in his eyes. She wanted to go to him, help him, but if they couldn't get inside, what hope was there?

Then she heard a familiar voice.

Her mother.

'Beth, sweetie, this isn't a good time. The adults are... talking.' There was a tremulous quality to her speech, like she was trying *very* hard to appear normal. 'Go home and... I'll see you in the morning.'

'No, you don't understand! It's—'

Music suddenly blared from unseen speakers, drowning her out, the volume dial cranked to ten.

'*Mum!*' roared Beth, her voice hoarse, fists slamming off the door. '*Mum!*'

They either couldn't hear her, or didn't care to. The music was deafening, and to make matters worse, it sounded like...James Blunt?

She looked at Grady, and a shimmering light caught her eye, emerging from behind Wok 'n' Roll, the abandoned Chinese take-away on the corner of the street. The glow danced like fireflies at night, restless and oddly beautiful. Her heart dropped into her stomach.

It was Maggie, fire dripping from her burning anatomy. Her body was aflame like a spectral suit of armour, only her head spared the torment by virtue of that absurdly long neck.

She smiled at them, and then she ran, heading straight for the town hall, each step leaving a flaming footprint. Beth spun back to the door, hammering her clenched fists until they were numb.

'Please! Let us in!'

They couldn't hear her. It was useless.

They were going to die here.

Maggie came at them like a guided missile. Forty yards away, then thirty. Grady was at the top of the steps now. Beth went to him, hoisting him up with all her strength, and together they pounded on the door.

The witch was so close she could feel the heat from the flames, hear her feet scratching along the tarmac. Grady stopped knocking.

'Beth,' he said sadly.

She turned to him, and he took her hand in his, their fingers entwining. Grady stooped slightly and kissed her, a kiss that tasted of blood and terror, and an understanding seemed to pass between them.

Maggie approached. They had seconds left.

Grady looked her in the eyes, putting his hands on her shoulders, his lower lip trembling.

'I love you,' he said, and then he shoved her backwards.

It all happened in slow motion.

Beth stumbled, tripping over a row of plant pots and landing on the grass an instant before Maggie hurtled into Grady, *through* him, his body liquefying before her eyes.

'*No!*' she cried, as the witch smashed through the door, and Grady's remains splashed over her face, his left arm and leg dropping onto the doorstep like parcels too big for the letterbox.

Then he was gone forever, another casualty of Maggie's insane rampage.

Beth wiped her sleeve across her face and it came away dark red with Grady's blood. It dripped down her face, her nose, her cheeks. She blinked away the crimson film over her eyes and stood, her whole body shaking.

She killed him. She killed Grady.

Without thinking, or perhaps guided by a primitive desire for vengeance, Beth staggered into the town hall. She froze in the doorway, unable to believe her eyes.

Or, more accurately, she didn't *want* to believe what she saw.

The room was a sea of writhing, naked bodies, indulging in every sexual act Beth could imagine, plus a few that she couldn't, and at least one that she wished she never knew existed. She took a deep breath, and the stale smell of sex filled her nostrils, choking her. Light-headed, she gripped the door frame for balance, her eyes darting across the acres of exposed flesh, the dripping fluids, the panting, red faces.

This wasn't a human sacrifice.

It was an orgy.

And in amongst the copulating bodies stood Maggie Wall, towering over the townspeople, fire coating her skeletal frame. The patterned curtains by the side of the door ignited, and at once the seething mass of bodies stopped fucking, staring in awed horror at Maggie's presence.

Beth's mother looked past the flaming demon and saw her only daughter standing in the doorway, watching, aghast. She pushed Charles Fredrikson away from her, his penis slopping out of her mouth, and moved to stand. Across the room, Beth's father, Donald, pulled out from Muriel Cockenzie and tried to cover his genitals.

Modesty was the least of his worries.

Maggie gazed around the room as the dying strains of James Blunt faded out, leaving a ponderous, echoing silence in its wake.

'Oh god, it's Maggie!' shouted someone.

'We're all going to fucking die!'

Then Barry White's *You're the First, the Last, My Everything* kicked in, and all hell broke loose.

Rod Hulme was the first casualty, Maggie's withered finger piercing the retired teacher's skull as he sat atop Theresa McKinally. A soupy paste of blood and brain matter exploded over Theresa's face, and she screamed until Maggie's foot came down on her head, crushing it like a grape.

Grinning inanely, Maggie took Sylvia Neilson by the neck. Maggie's hands, like the rest of her, were still aflame. Sylvia's face went red, then purple, then black, her eyeballs melting and dribbling down her cheeks, sizzling as they did so. Maggie tossed her aside and stepped fully forwards.

Nude bodies dived and scrambled to escape. Clive Moonie ran for the windows, knocking Karen Collins to one side, treading on her, her ribs cracking under his dirty bare feet. He grappled with the shutter, penis flopping as he did so, but it was locked. They all were.

Razor-sharp talons shredded Clive's back easily, as Maggie forced her hand into his body, grasping his spinal column. The bones crumbled in her grip and Clive collapsed in a heap, spitting blood, landing on top of Evelyn Ronald, who, at eighty-three, was the oldest participant in the ritual. Evelyn held her fingers in a cross shape, and Maggie brushed the old woman's hands aside and clawed her throat out, holding the chunk of mauled flesh in her over-sized hand.

'Beth,' roared Donald Collins, still cupping one hand over his erection. Maggie knocked him down and grabbed him by the feet. She lifted Beth's father, then slammed him back onto the ground. Muriel Cockenzie was there to break his fall, their heads smashing together, skulls cracking at the same instant. Shirley Bannatyne made her escape, but Maggie spotted her, swinging Donald's lifeless body like a baseball bat. The corpse smacked into her chest, and Shirley fell, landing on a patch of burning yoga mat. She rolled helplessly across it, the flames scalding her. When she sat up, wailing in agony, most of her skin was still stuck to the mat, peeling away and exposing the raw, glistening muscle beneath.

The fire spread quickly. The mats had sat untouched in the storeroom since the Great Auchenmullan Yoga Craze of '93, and the highly flammable material was ablaze within seconds.

Inspector Carlisle stood near the podium, where he and Johnny Huston had been spit-roasting Janet Rob, whose now-deceased mother had once dated Carlisle back in the early seventies.

The policeman roughly withdrew his cock and raced for the pile of neatly folded clothes placed along the perimeter. The cavernous acoustics of the hall amplified the screams as bodies hurtled through the air, some on fire, some broken messes. Carlisle, his erection still strong, fumbled for his leather belt, where he had a small firearm tucked. It was not legal, but there had been no one to complain, and it made him feel like a real man when he carried it. He raised the pistol and squared the barrel at Maggie Wall, devil-witch from Hell.

Some of the townsfolk had laughed at him behind his back for carrying a gun.

Dirty Larry, they had called him.

'Who's laughing now?' he sneered as he closed one eye and lined up the shot. Maggie had Thomas Pierce in both hands, her mouth widening, shoving his head in-between rows of yellowing, razor-like teeth.

Carlisle pulled the trigger.

The bullet hit Pierce in the left buttock, and he roared in agony just as Maggie chomped down, severing his head from his neck in one motion. She spat the head out, where it rolled across the floor and bumped into the steaming, disembowelled corpse of June Trotter.

Carlisle took aim and fired again. As he did, he slid on the blood-slaked floor and the bullet flew wide, catching Beth's mother in the neck. Arterial spray jetted from the wound. She staggered towards her daughter, looking at her through the rising flames. The blood gushed like a crimson rainbow, spraying the walls, and she collapsed dead along-side the others.

Beth watched all this in stunned, anaesthetised silence.

What she was witnessing wasn't just impossible...it was an abomination.

Someone — it looked to her like Sally Prentiss, a pharmacy worker in Inverness — ran for the burning door. She jumped towards Beth through the flames, but at the last second a screaming man bumped into her, knocking her off course. She fell, grabbing the curtains and ripping them from the rail, the blazing fabric landing atop her, cloaking her nude body.

Finding the strength to act, Beth stepped in, wrenching the curtains from the woman. Their pattern — gold rings and crosses — was burnt onto Sally's skin, her lustrous blonde hair replaced by dark, smouldering curls.

Beth recoiled from the overpowering stench of burning meat as Sally sizzled like a burger on a grill. She stepped backwards, and that was when she heard her name.

'Beth!'

It was a voice drenched in unimaginable horror, and it took her a moment to recognise it.

Through the smoke, she saw the source. Her best friend...*crucified*.

'Alice!' she shouted. She was still alive...thank god she was *still alive*.

Beth didn't have time to think. She ducked beneath the flaming entrance, already picking out the safest route to the stage. The mats were burning, but there was just enough space by the far wall to make it.

She hoped.

Groping, desperate hands grabbed at her as she deftly dodged between the mats, trying to stick to the wall. Through the black smoke, she could make out Maggie tearing someone apart. A severed arm splattered the wall in front of her, and Beth ignored it.

Once you've seen a witch tear a man inside out from his arsehole, you've seen it all.

Barry White crooned over the sounds of screaming, the CD player miraculously unharmed by the fire. She vaulted onto the stage, racing towards Alice, bumping into a wicker basket as she did so. The basket wobbled, and started to topple.

'Eric!' yelled Alice, and somehow Beth reached out and caught the handle. She exchanged a shocked glance with Alice, then put the basket beside the cross, Eric shrieking in confusion. She worked the knots loose as the fire finally reached the CD player, putting Barry White out of his misery. The last cord dropped to the floor, and Alice fell forward on stiff legs, picking up Eric and hugging him.

The dreadful wails of the dying resonated throughout the hall as a monstrous figure lumbered through the smoke towards them.

Maggie emerged in all her infernal glory. She stared at them both, her head swaying.

'My...baby,' she said, and grinned even wider.

Carlisle glanced around the room.

He appeared to be the last man standing. He trod on corpses with every step, covering his mouth with his hand, trying not to breathe in the noxious fumes of the burning yoga mats. To his right, beyond the sea of human remains, was the exit. He could escape, if he wanted. The baby belonged to Maggie now.

Her revenge had been sweet.

Auchenmullan lay in ruins, the people dead, the prophecy fulfilled. If only he had acted sooner. Christ, he had tried to, but those squabbling buffoons had too many questions. They had lost faith in the old ways.

Their ancestors would be mortified.

Now here he was, the sole survivor of the massacre. Maggie would take the baby and return to the mountain, and Carlisle would never see her again. He took a tentative step towards the doorway and stopped, the gun hot in his hand.

That bitch Maggie had destroyed everything he held dear. This town was *his* town, dammit. It wasn't hers to take! He was the law around here.

Dirty fuckin' *Larry*.

'Not this time,' he snarled, stomping back over the bodies of his friends and neighbours.

He had a witch to kill.

'*My...baby,*' hissed Maggie, her cracked tongue blackened by the flames, teeth red with the blood of Auchenmullan.

Beth's eyes scanned the stage for a weapon. There was some sort of ceremonial dagger next to the wicker Moses basket, but it would do no real damage to the behemoth before her. Alice retreated, cradling Eric, and Beth stepped between them and the witch.

'What...the *fuck*...is that?' said Alice, and Beth remembered this was the first time Alice had seen Maggie. There was no time to explain. There had to be another way out. She knew she should be terrified, or preparing for her death, but she was too...*angry*. Yes, that was it. She was angry. Furious. This *thing* had killed Grady. It had killed her parents. And now it wanted her best friend too?

Maggie reached out towards them, and Beth found her

eyes drawn to that maddening hole in her belly. The blood inside bubbled, pouring out in frenzied torrents.

'Stay away from her!' screamed Beth.

Maggie raised one hand, the long, tapered fingers tightening into rigid claws, ready to strike. There was a deafening report, and a bullet tore through Maggie's chest, slamming into the wooden cross two inches wide of Beth's head.

Maggie wheezed, viscous yellow goo dribbling from the small hole, and turned to face her attacker. Lawrence Carlisle stepped naked from between the flames, the gun locked firmly on its target.

'Why'd you come back, Maggie?' he shouted.

She said nothing, and he circled her. 'This child isn't from here. She's not yours to take. This *town* is not yours to take.' He fired. One shot. Two, three, four, pulling the trigger until the hammer punched down on an empty chamber. The bullets rippled through her, blowing out dust and bone fragments.

Maggie's head swooped down towards Carlisle, coming face-to-face with him. He stared into her nightmarish visage.

'All...my...babies,' she whispered.

Carlisle shook his head. 'She's not yours.' Out of the corner of his eye, he saw Beth leap from the stage, Alice handing her the baby and following.

My god, he thought. They were still alive. There was hope yet.

Carlisle smiled at Maggie.

'Well then, you dried up old cunt,' he said. 'What the fuck are you waiting for?'

Maggie's traced her nails delicately down the sides of his head, slicing the skin. He pulled the trigger instinctively, over and over, as her talons dug into his face, cutting around his features until she had enough loose skin to grasp in both hands. Then she wrenched the flesh from Carlisle's face, discarding the soft tissue in the fire. He screamed as Maggie dug her nails into his chest, scratching against the bone, snapping ribs out of the way one at a time.

'Do it,' he roared, somehow still alive. 'Just fucking do it!'

'All...my...babies,' she said, as she ripped Carlisle's heart from his chest and held the still-beating organ up before him.

His screams echoed across the valley...and then they echoed no more.

26

THE COLLINS FAMILY NISSAN WAS PARKED OUT FRONT, THE doors unlocked, the keys dangling in the ignition.

Beth was not surprised by this. Her parents were nothing if not predictable.

Her parents...

They were dead now. Everyone was. The whole damn town. And what they had been doing in there, that ritual... that *orgy*...

She pushed the thought aside, unwilling to dwell on it, and climbed into the car. Alice and Eric got in alongside her, and as the door slammed they were off, the hall a shrinking beacon of light in the rearview mirror, plumes of black smoke rising skyward. Neither of them spoke, their thoughts too dreadful to verbalise. Alice rolled down her window, letting the freezing air swirl through the car. White frost coated the pavements and the trees like the inside of an unshaken snow globe.

They passed a nude man crawling on all fours, his hand pressed to his stomach. It was Frank Mason, part-time post-man. He must have escaped, and now his guts spilled out between splayed fingers, slopping onto the ground. He didn't seem to notice them, and Beth kept on driving.

Part of her wanted to swerve onto the pavement and listen to the crunch of his bones beneath the tyres. He would have killed Alice, or at least been privy to it. Let him die. Let him fucking die along with the rest of them. They all deserved it.

All except—

'Grady's dead,' said Beth. The words hung like slabs of rotten meat. 'Steve too.'

Alice nodded, cradling Eric. She couldn't stop staring at him, touching him. When she looked up at Beth, her face was ashen and drawn. 'That thing...was that...'

'Yeah,' said Beth quickly. 'That was her.'

She filled Alice in on the evening's events as best she could, though it was like describing a dream, portions of it fading from her mind as she spoke. Perhaps one day she would forget it entirely, and lie alone in a care home, senile and forsaken and blissfully unencumbered by the burden of memory.

She took a corner too fast, the wheels skidding across the slippery road, and slowed to thirty. One car crash was quite enough for today. She could still feel it in her stiff neck and bruised shoulders. Once they left town and hit the motorway, then they could speed up.

They cruised by Alice's house. The lights were on, but Alice didn't notice. Her attention was focused on Eric.

'She's come for him, hasn't she?' said Alice.

'Yeah.'

There was no point lying.

Beth looked out the window, at the empty houses blurring by, where once had lived families with hopes and dreams, but now sat unloved and left to ruin. They passed the closed-down pet store, its windows boarded up, and the garage, and the pitiful point-of-interest St Mary's Hump. She remembered staring in the pet store window for hours as a kid, looking at the poster of a strange flat-faced dog with the saddest expression she'd ever seen.

'They asked me all these questions,' said Alice, stroking her finger lovingly down Eric's round face, her voice faraway sounding. 'About where Eric was born, where Kevin and I had sex. I thought they were all crazy. They were going to kill him.'

'And you too,' said Beth, still picturing the dog on the poster, the pug that had seemed to encapsulate her feelings in a single look.

Alice shrugged. 'I didn't care about me. I really didn't. At that moment, I realised something. I'd give up my life for him. Isn't that funny? I would rather *die* than let anything happen to him. Can you understand that?'

'You love him,' said Beth. The traffic lights were at red, but she drove straight through.

Sorry, Larry.

'It's more than that,' said Alice. 'He *is* me. The better part of me.' She smiled humourlessly. 'For now, at least. He's not been tainted by the world. Right now he's pure and perfect and everything that's good.'

'I guess we were like that once,' said Beth.

'Yeah. Then we grew up and gave our parents a real hard time. You ever regret it?'

'Never really thought about it.'

'I think about it all the time now, how I used to stay out all night, coming home in the morning to find my mum sitting up in the chair, worried sick. I never realised how much she must have cared. I should have, but I never stopped to think. I guess you don't, as a kid.'

Beth nodded. The smell of Eric's unchanged nappy lingered unpleasantly in the car.

She felt Alice's hand on her leg.

'Thank you,' said Alice.

'For what?'

'You came back for me,' she said. 'You could have left, but you didn't. You saved Eric's life.'

'You're my best friend,' said Beth. 'You would have done the same.'

Would she, though? If it came down to it, and it was between protecting Eric or saving Beth, would Alice leave her? Would she run?

Of course she would. Can you blame her?

Alice was right. There was a love, a bond, between her and Eric that Beth could never comprehend. She had never wanted to be a mother. Why would she want to bring another miserable life into the world...into Auchenmullan?

Not that it mattered anymore. The town as they knew it ceased to exist. Only her, Alice, and Eric remained. Auchenmullan was gone, and with it the inhabitants, wiped from the Earth in one fell swoop. In a way, it was what she had always wanted. She had no reason to return, not now, not ever.

But she also had nowhere to go. Despite everything, her whole world was wrapped up in this rotten little town.

The turnoff to Spectre Loch whizzed by, and she thought of Grady, of that night by the loch, the air alive with mating dragonflies, the moon reflecting off the ripples in the water. They had lain naked by the shore, entangled in each other's arms, her head resting on Grady's chest. He had told her he loved her, and she had responded with an embarrassed *thank you*.

Gone. All gone.

She hadn't told him she loved him often enough. Her parents, too.

But it was too late to do anything about that. Wasn't it always?

She glanced in the wing mirror and saw no trace of the witch. At least now she was easy to spot.

Eight feet tall and on fire. Put that *on the police bulletin.*

Where *were* the police? It had been over an hour since Jack had spoken to them on the phone. Maybe they weren't coming. Would that be so bad? How many more lives needed to be lost to quench Maggie's bloodlust? She had a sudden crazed urge to spin the car round and drive back to town, right into Maggie's waiting arms.

Let her take them. They had nothing left to offer.

Speak for yourself.

'How do we stop her?' said Alice, startling Beth. The car veered into the middle of the road, and she eased it back again. They were nearing the edge of town, and from here the road became a single-lane country track for several miles.

'I'm not sure we can,' said Beth.

She hadn't meant to be so honest, but what was she supposed to say? Maggie had been shot, blown up, set on fire...nothing stopped her. She was like the killer in some dumb slasher movie.

'Maybe if we get out of town...'

'Yeah, maybe,' agreed Beth, though deep down, she didn't believe it. She wanted to, so badly, but what if Maggie kept following them? If they made it to Inverness, or even one of the nearby villages, and brought Maggie with them, the carnage would be devastating. They couldn't live their lives on the run. Alice said nothing, and Beth assumed she was thinking the same thing.

They drove on, a low mist sweeping down from the mountains. Auchenmullan was behind them now, and a white sign appeared through the trees like a ghost. Beth knew what was printed on the other side of it.

WELCOME TO AUCHENMULLAN
PLEASE DRIVE CAREFULLY

Spray-painted over the bottom three words was —

YOU'LL NEVER LEAVE

She didn't know who had painted that slogan, but it had been there for years. Once, it had even seemed funny, rather than a grim prophecy.

'Almost there,' whispered Alice.

'How's Eric?'

'He's sleeping.' Alice held his tiny hand, and he gurgled.

The welcome sign flashed past, and then was gone, replaced by a dark wall of Caledonian pine trees that stretched to the horizon. Beth pressed the accelerator, the speedometer nudging fifty as they raced through the night on a road to nowhere.

'Are we still friends?' said Alice.

The words pierced Beth's heart and she almost lost control of the vehicle. She gripped the wheel so hard that pain seared up her arms.

'Why would you say that?'

Alice wouldn't even look at her. 'It's just I've not seen you since I had Eric.'

'I've...'

What, exactly? I've been busy? No one's gonna believe that lie.

A sign for the old sawmill shot by, dented and faded. Once they were past the mill road, they were really out of town.

And then what?

The snow was coming down heavily, and Beth switched on the windscreen wipers. They struggled to keep up, the white flakes accumulating on the glass.

'You don't need to say anything,' said Alice, a little too sharply. 'I understand. You think things have changed between us. Well guess what? They have. I have a son now, so like it or not, my whole life *has* changed forever.'

'I know.'

'Do you? We never see each other anymore. You visited me once in the hospital, and once since I got home.'

'Twice,' corrected Beth, before realising that wasn't much better. She glanced through the snow-streaked window. There was a dark shape on the road.

'Al, there's something up ahead,' she said.

'Don't change the subject. You always do this!'

The snow whipped up into a blizzard, the wipers working overtime.

'What *is* that?' said Beth. Alice kept talking, and Beth wanted to shake her and tell her to shut the fuck up. This was not the time for a lecture.

A faint light glowed...flickering...flashing...

It couldn't be.

'You know what I think, Beth?' continued Alice. 'I think you're *scared* of leaving Auchenmullan. I think—'

'*Hold on!*'

She hit the brakes, and the car skidded. Alice screamed, gripping on to Eric, as Beth slammed the wheel hard to the left, trying to keep them steady. The Nissan spun as Beth lost control, and she frantically jerked the wheel the other way, attempting to course-correct, no longer sure which direction they were facing.

The car slowed, then gently struck a wooden fencepost and came to a stop.

Alice clutched at Beth's arm. 'What is it? Is it her?'

'No,' she said, heart thumping in her chest, hands trembling.

It wasn't Maggie. She was fast, but she couldn't have gotten ahead of them.

'So what is it?' said Alice. She sounded hysterical. 'You almost crashed! We could have died.'

Beth took a deep breath. It was the only thing *worse* than Maggie.

'It's the police,' she said.

'Then we're safe,' whispered Alice. 'They can protect us.'

'You think they can stop her? You saw what Larry's gun did to her. Nothing.'

'But—'

'No,' said Beth. 'We need to keep going. We don't have time to stop.'

Someone was trudging towards them through the snow, holding their hand up to shield their eyes.

'Let me do the talking,' said Beth. 'If we stay here, we're dead.'

'Maybe we've lost her?'

'You believe that?'

Alice said nothing.

A light rap at Beth's window made them both jump.

A burly police officer in a hi-vis jacket peered in, frost clinging to his beard. Behind him, two squad cars formed a roadblock across the only route out of town. Normally they would have been easy to spot, but the snow flurry had rendered them almost invisible. Beth rolled down her window.

'Going pretty fast there, weren't you?' said the officer, raising his voice above the howling gale that swept through the valley. He flashed his warrant card at them. PC Blackwood, it said. In the photo ID he was clean-shaven and serious looking.

'You have to let us past, she's chasing us,' blurted Alice.

Beth silently cursed. That kind of talk did them no favours.

'Aye, sure,' he said, like an adult humouring a child.

'I'm sorry, officer,' said Beth, trying to stay cool. 'We're in a hurry. Her baby's sick, and we need to get him to a hospital.'

He looked intently at Beth. 'You come from Auchenmullan?'

'Yes,' said Beth. 'Listen, we—'

'That *your* baby?' he asked, looking at Alice.

She nodded. 'We need to get him to safety.'

'To *hospital*,' corrected Beth.

Fuck's sake, keep quiet!

The officer glanced from face to face. 'Noticed you didn't have your snow tyres on.'

'We didn't have time,' said Beth, glancing in the mirror again and seeing nothing but endless white. 'We're in a hurry.'

'You keep checking your mirror,' said Blackwood. 'Looking for anything in particular?'

Yes, a witch. A giant fucking witch. Now let us pass.

'Well,' said Beth, the lie taking shape, 'We almost crashed into you because of the snow. I don't want another car to—'

But Blackwood wasn't interested. He waved a dismissive

hand, and Beth stopped talking. 'Wait in the vehicle, please,' he said, and walked away, the snow enveloping him.

Beth turned to Alice. 'I said let *me* do the talking!' she said. She closed her fingers around the steering wheel and glanced in the mirror for a sign of Maggie. It was becoming an obsession. Squinting through the frosty glass, she saw the officer leaning into one of the vehicles. There were at least two more cops with him.

Come on, come on, come on...

Questions darted through her mind. What was taking him so long? Were these the cops Jack had called, and if so, what had he told them? She clenched her jaw so hard her teeth hurt.

'That's it,' she said, 'I'm getting us out of here.'

'Beth!'

'You got a better idea, now's the time.'

She turned the key, the engine springing into life as the doors to the squad cars burst open and three officers came racing towards them. The wheels of the Nissan spun hopelessly on the icy road. 'Fuck!' said Beth, banging her fists off the wheel. 'Fuck, fuck, fuck!'

That cop was right about one thing, she thought. *Shouldn't be out without snow tyres.*

'Out of the vehicle,' shouted Blackwood. 'Now!'

'What do we do?' cried Alice.

'I don't know!' Beth killed the engine. She was all out of ideas.

A young female officer yanked her door open and dragged her from the car. Beth fought, lashing out with her fists, but the woman overpowered her, forcing her onto the road and pressing her face against the freezing tarmac.

'Careful with the baby,' she heard Blackwood shout.

What was happening with Alice? Beth could see nothing

but the shoes of the two officers beneath the body of the car. She felt the female cop's knee on her back.

'You're under arrest,' said the woman, closely followed by the metallic rattle of handcuffs.

'No, you don't understand,' cried Beth. Maggie could arrive any minute, but how could she make them believe her? The police were not exactly world-renowned for their imagination. They'd think she was drunk, or high, or whatever was easiest to write up in their report.

She had to escape. It was her only chance.

Beth lay still while the cop fumbled with the cuffs, letting her think she'd given up. The pressure on her spine relaxed, and she wrestled one arm free, pushing up from the ground with surprising strength. The cop slid off her, landing on her back, and Beth struggled to her feet on the frozen road. The cop followed, clutching the handcuffs in one hand, reaching for her baton with the other. She drew the weapon.

Beth knew she had to act fast.

She lunged forwards. Surprised, the cop dodged to the side, slipping on the ice, a bewildered expression coming over her as she fell. Her head struck the edge of the car door with a wet *smack*, and she hit the ground hard. Beth looked down at the woman lying motionless at her feet.

You did that.

The woman's leg jittered and twitched. She couldn't be much older than Beth.

You killed her.

'Officer down!' shouted Blackwood. His partner — an older woman — held Alice's arms behind her back. Inside the car, on the passenger seat, Eric sobbed.

'I didn't touch her!' said Beth, staring in horrified fascination at the blood that seeped from the cop's head, flowing out across the ice.

Blackwood made his way round the vehicle, his own feet sliding. 'Cuff that bitch,' he shouted to his partner, and seconds later Beth heard the brutal sound of handcuffs snapping onto Alice's wrists.

Beth held her hands up. 'I swear, I never—'

'Shut up!' roared Blackwood. He reached Beth, brought his baton crashing down on her shoulder. The pain was immense, rattling her bones from her toes to her teeth. She backed away from him, tears frozen in the corners of her eyes.

'I'm sorry, I'm sorry' she kept repeating. Blackwood glanced down at the prone officer, kneeling to put two fingers to her neck. He glared at Beth.

'You little...'

Something seemed to catch his eye. He looked beyond Beth, almost *through* her, his eyes narrowing.

'What the fuck is that?' he said, lowering his baton.

If the temperature wasn't already hovering around zero, it would have sent a shiver down Beth's spine.

'We have to get out of here,' she said.

Blackwood didn't seem to hear her.

'Hey, Wise,' he called to his partner. 'You see that?'

The other cop walked slowly round and stood by his side.

Beth didn't want to turn, didn't want to *look*, but she had to know. She had to be sure. She pivoted carefully on the ice and gazed down the road. Far away, in the middle of the blank, colourless landscape, a bright light burned through the snow.

'Is that a lorry?' said Blackwood.

'Not quite,' said Beth. She watched the demented

blazing madness swirl through the heavy sleet, closing the distance.

Blackwood's partner looked at Beth. 'Get in the car,' she said. 'And get your friend in too.'

'What *is* that?' said Blackwood.

'We need to leave,' said Beth. 'She'll kill us all.'

'What are you talking about?'

'I can't explain, just *get us the fuck out of here!*'

He pushed past her and raised a radio to his lips. 'This is PC Blackwood on, uh, Old Mill Road. We need backup. Officer down, and there's...something...'

Beth made her way round to Alice. Her friend lay face down, wrists cuffed behind her back, her loose white dress soaked through. Her skin was red and sore from the biting cold. Beth helped her stand, Eric crying beside them in the relative comfort of the car.

The fearsome light moved closer, growing larger as it advanced.

Alice stared at Beth. 'What do we do?' she said.

Beth thought hard. They were in the middle of nowhere. The nearest town was Kingussie, but they couldn't make it in this weather, not on foot. There was nowhere left to run. Well, apart from—

'The mill,' she said. 'It's our only chance.'

Alice looked like she wanted to argue, and Beth couldn't blame her. The mill had partially burnt down years ago. It was a dilapidated deathtrap, a place where the young folk of Auchenmullan used to go to get up to mischief — drugs, sex, and general fooling around.

There was nothing there to protect them from a monster, but at least it was better than the alternative — waiting here for Maggie to rip them apart.

Alice locked eyes with Beth.

'You need to carry Eric,' she said.

Shit.

She leaned into the car and gingerly lifted the infant. It was the first time she had ever held a baby, and it felt unnatural. She tried to emulate the way Alice cradled him, supporting his head and back, keeping him close to her.

The two remaining officers stood side-by-side, drawing their batons, not noticing as Beth and Alice slipped away with the baby, sneaking into the trees.

Beth led the way, treading carefully. Eric looked up at her and she tried to smile at him. Behind her, Alice's footsteps crunched softly in the snow. Maggie would be here soon. Those cops didn't stand a chance.

You tried to warn them.

True. But they didn't listen, the same way she wouldn't have listened had someone told her that the legend of Maggie Wall was true.

It struck her that modern life was people talking, talking, talking, and no one really listening. She was as guilty of it as anyone.

Her feet sank in the snow, making it hard to walk. Still, the sawmill wasn't too far. They would get there before Maggie.

And after that?

Beth had no idea.

27

PC Norma Wise readied her weapon.

The baton felt weightless in her hand, insubstantial. She turned to PC Keith Blackwood, her partner for the last two years, and said, 'That's no car. That's a person.'

'Bollocks,' said Blackwood. 'It's too big...too fast.'

Norma looked over her shoulder, at the body of PC Trisha Ramsey lying slumped in the snow. She was still breathing. Norma wanted to go to the younger woman, to check on her, to put her in the car and drive her to the hospital, but she was rooted to the spot. A memory, long-suppressed, clawed its way through the dirt of her mind.

'Those girls have gone,' said Blackwood.

'Let them go. We've found who we're looking for.'

Blackwood turned to her, the yellow light on the road growing brighter and brighter. 'But we were told—'

'I know why we're here, Keith. Better than you ever could.'

He didn't press her for details, and Norma was thankful for that. Reliving the memory of that day was a painful and traumatic experience, and one she avoided at all costs. It usually came to her on the long winter nights, when she sat alone in her flat with too much wine, the wind battering the windows. Now, it appeared to be unavoidable, and all because they had been stuck in roadworks on the High Street of Aviemore.

She had been sitting alongside Blackwood in the police cruiser outside Tesco, dozens of gridlocked cars tooting their horns in an atonal cacophony, when the transmission screeched over the airwaves. It came from a squad car sent to Auchenmullan after a call from a man ranting about murders, and death, and a baby. If Norma got out of this alive, she knew those words would haunt her til the end of her days.

'Is there anybody there?' the voice had said.

'This is despatch, please identify yourself.'

'They're dead...they're all dead.'

'Calm down and identify yourself.'

'She's back, my god, she's back! She wants her baby!'

'Ma'am, are you a police officer?'

'No, they're dead! She tore them apart. She fucking ripped them up and tore them apart!'

The transmission ended with a throat-rending scream, cutting out midway through. Moments later, they received the official call to head to Auchenmullan, where they rendezvoused with another vehicle to form a roadblock and await further instruction.

When the girls came along, Blackwood had smiled and said they had gotten lucky. Two females, one carrying a baby. They fit the loose description, and yet Wise thought otherwise. She hoped to God in heaven that he was right, and bit her tongue. Blackwood was unaware that Norma had grown up in Auchenmullan. He didn't know that she had still lived there in the summer of nineteen-eighty-five, when Maggie Wall had descended the mountain with vengeance in her shattered heart.

And he certainly never know she had come face-to-face with the beast and lived to tell the tale, an experience that had driven Norma from the cursed town forever. This was as close as she had gotten to Auchenmullan in the ensuing years. When she heard the transmission, part of her hoped it was a joke, but deep down, she knew otherwise.

'You ever hear about Maggie Wall?' she asked Blackwood, unsurprised by the tremor in her voice.

'Can't say I have,' he said. 'Why?'

Norma swallowed back her words. 'No reason,' she said, and wiped snow from her eyes.

The light was getting closer. Much closer. Norma squinted, shielding her vision with her free hand, the snowflakes sticking to her lashes.

'She's back,' she said, and it was true.

Maggie Wall had returned.

It was the silhouette that gave her away. Inhumanly tall and thin, the juddering movements, and the way her head swayed atop that neck...

Norma said a silent prayer and thought of her husband and son, and how she wished she had been able to say goodbye to them.

'Is this fucker on fire?' said Blackwood, his voice shaking with disbelief.

'I'd say so, Keith.'

She didn't know what to do. At that moment, rational thought deserted her the way she had deserted Auchenmullan thirty-four years ago. Maggie lumbered towards them through the snow, her limbs creaking as she walked, fire blackening her stiff body.

'Get in the car,' said Norma, as the fiery horror advanced.

'What *is* that?' shuddered Blackwood. He looked at his baton, as if willing it to transform into a gun, or — better yet — a bazooka.

'Get in the car, *now*.'

'Jesus Christ,' was all Blackwood could say.

Norma left him standing there, darting for the vehicle as fast as the ice would allow. She had a *family*. If Blackwood wanted to die, then that was his decision. She wasn't his mother, for God's sake.

Footsteps pounded, gaining on her. She heard Keith scream and kept her head down, closing in on the cars. It was too late for him, but she could still survive. The coldness of her thoughts appalled her. Keith had a family too, didn't he? A girlfriend, at least, a bonnie wee lass called Mary.

Now was not the time to think like that. She reached the nearest cruiser and threw herself in, grasping for the keys. The engine roared into life right as Blackwood crashed into the windscreen, his belly open, intestines pressed up against the shattered glass. Norma, a seasoned veteran of the police force who was not prone to screaming, did just that. Trembling with fear, she stabbed at the accelerator with numb feet, the snow-tyres catching on the ice, the vehicle lurching forwards. She tried to steer, but Blackwood's body obscured her vision. Norma leaned out the window, trying to grab at his sleeve, to haul him off the car, and as she did so, the front of the vehicle crunched through the metal safety barrier and briefly became airborne. She was still desperately groping for her seatbelt when the car struck the ground at an angle. It balanced a second, almost vertical, and then tipped forwards onto its roof.

The vehicle slid down the embankment, running over Blackwood's body with a wet squelching sound, Norma rattling around inside like a human pinball. By the time it stopped, she had broken damn-near every bone in her body.

The car came to rest by the side of a frozen stream, smoke billowing from under the bonnet. She couldn't feel her limbs, and it was probably for the best.

Lying there like a rag-doll, she listened as the radio crackled.

'This is despatch, do you copy?'

Norma willed her hand to move. If she could just reach the radio to call for an ambulance, or for backup, or...

An ominous, otherworldly heat prickled her skin. Unable to turn around, she knew where it was coming from.

'This is despatch, do you copy?'

I'm right here, she wanted to say. *Maggie's back! Maggie's back! Maggie's—*

Then a skeletal hand closed over her face and dragged her from the car.

She was dead long before Maggie was finished with her.

28

BETH HADN'T REALISED HOW HEAVY BABIES WERE.

But then, she'd never had to hold one while running for her life through a midnight forest, the needles of the pine trees scratching at her face, the snow blinding her. Alice lagged behind, trying to keep up and failing, her wrists cuffed. All she wore was the baggy white ceremonial dress, and the fabric kept snagging on the outstretched branches. Beth paused, waiting for her.

'Keep going,' shouted Alice breathlessly.

'You okay?'

'Don't worry about me. Keep Eric safe.'

'I will,' said Beth, though she was tiring, her movements lethargic. She thought back to just a few hours ago, drinking in the bowling alley. She had sobered up pretty quickly since then.

Death has a funny way of doing that.

You wanted excitement.

Not like this. Never like this.

Eric grumbled unhappily in her arms. He was so small, so precious, and she worried she was holding him too tight.

What was that book Mr Ryden had made them read in high school, the one where the guy hugs the little girl too hard and kills her? She couldn't recall. She had spent most of that term passing notes to Grady under the desk. One time, she had even let him put his hand up her skirt in class.

Focus, dammit!

It was difficult. Faced with death, all she could do was reminisce. Was this what happened when you knew you were going to die?

Nostalgia ain't what it used to be.

She used to say that a lot, and Grady would laugh, and Steve would complain that he didn't get it. He was such an idiot, sometimes. A big, dead idiot.

Up ahead, two large structures wrestled their way above the trees.

The twin smokestacks of the sawmill.

Almost there.

She knew this area well, had spent many summer evenings here with friends. Throughout her childhood the chimneys had belched white smoke constantly, and her father had told her they were the cigarettes of giants who lay sleeping under the earth.

Your father is dead now.

True, but there was nothing she could do about that. If — *when* — she got out of this, she would have time to grieve, to mourn. She would probably hate them for a while, for the humiliating way they had died, but that feeling would undoubtedly pass.

'It's just ahead,' she called to Alice.

The trees were thinning, the mill looming large, its once impeccable pinewood exterior now a charred shell. A single car sat out front, belonging to one of the workers who had lost his life in the fire. Its tyres were flat, the windows smashed, the body dented and bruised. It reminded Beth of the bodies people found in forests in those true crime documentaries, except nobody was coming to claim this one.

She chanced a glance back. No sign of Maggie.

But she would be following. She was *always* following. Beth understood that there was no escape. Maggie would follow them to the ends of the Earth, her bloodlust insatiable.

Well, that wasn't true, was it? Maggie's bloodlust could be sated rather easily. Very, *very* easily indeed.

By handing over the baby.

No!

She couldn't think that. It wasn't even an option. She would *die* before she let that happen.

A perimeter fence circled the mill, seven-feet high and topped with strands of barbed wire. There was a bird ensnared in the grip of the metal, thin guts hanging frozen from its stomach.

Beth was unconcerned by the fence. It was riddled with holes from animals and curious teens. The first time she had gone, there had been twenty of them, and the night had ended in chaos when the police arrived and accompanied the teens back to their homes. Well, the ones that got caught, anyway. Beth recalled hiding behind some industrial machinery with Grady, her heart beating through her chest, while he had held her close and told her everything would be okay. At the time, it was the closest she had ever been to a boy. When the police departed, Grady had walked her home hand-in-hand. Under the soft light of her porch, they had kissed for the first time, midges swarming around their heads, biting their skin, neither of them caring. She must have been fourteen or fifteen, her body tingling with the intoxication of young love, and also, of course, plenty of Buckfast.

She veered right, heading in the direction of the gated entrance to the mill's grounds. Where was she going? What was the plan?

She didn't have one, and presumed Alice didn't either.

'What about you?' she asked the crying bundle. Eric responded by letting out a piercing wail.

There! A hole in the fence. Beth knelt and shoved Eric through a little too roughly. His cries became louder. She looked back and saw Alice trailing behind, her face streaked with tears, her nose gushing blood.

'What happened?' asked Beth.

'I fell,' said Alice, as Beth pulled the fence apart like a magician revealing a trick, creating enough room for Alice to slip through on her knees, her face pressing into the snow and leaving a crimson trail. Beth followed, scooping up Eric and jogging through the overgrown grass and weeds that had burst up through the concrete of the old carpark. The mill itself was mostly intact, or at least it looked that way from ground level. Most of the roof was gone, a casualty of the blaze that had ravaged the mill and left it a stark, hollowed-out reminder of Auchenmullan's prosperous past.

Beth looked over her shoulder. All she could see was thick, murky darkness flecked with transient white snowflakes. No flaming witch rampaging through the trees, no ungodly shrieks.

Nothing.

'Where is she?' said Alice. 'Have we lost her?'

'I don't know,' said Beth quietly. 'Maybe the police stopped her?'

'They're dead,' said Alice, to which Beth had no reply.

The main door swung lazily on its hinges. They ducked

beneath the flapping DO NOT ENTER police tape and entered the old reception area. The glass panel at the welcome desk was broken, as was the screen of the computer behind it. A squirrel peeked out from the monitor, regarding them with suspicion. Snow and pine cones coated the floor, the desk, the chair, like some kind of frozen hell. A portrait of Albert Montgomery gazed down from the walls through a cracked and spider-webbed frame. He had founded the mill in the sixties. Now, the poor bastard was condemned to watch his legacy crumble to dust for all eternity.

They wandered the snow-covered corridors, going nowhere in particular, just walking, deeper into the belly of the mill, away from Maggie, or perhaps closer, neither of them knew for sure. At every corner they paused, stricken with the fear that she would be there, waiting, blood dripping from gore-encrusted fingernails, lips pulled back in that ghastly, toothy smile.

But she never was.

It was almost, in a macabre way, disappointing. There were piles of wood, and empty offices, and sawdust — so much sawdust — but no Maggie Wall.

Eric continued to cry.

'Why won't he stop?' asked Beth.

'He's hungry,' said Alice. She looked at Beth with pleading, wet eyes. 'Help me feed him.'

'Oh, I don't think—'

'We might die here, Beth,' she said. The words echoed down long-untrodden corridors and out into the stillness of the forest.

There was a silence before Beth said, 'I know.'

'So help me, please. Help me feed my son. It might be the last—'

'Okay. Just don't say...' Beth swallowed, and felt like crying. '...what you were about to say.'

Alice slumped against the wall and slid to a sitting position. Beth laid Eric in Alice's lap and unbuttoned the large brown buttons of the dress. The way Alice looked at her infant son, lying there helpless, broke her heart. She undid the last button, revealing Alice's maternity bra.

'It just unfastens,' said Alice. 'The cup, I mean.'

Beth nodded, following Alice's orders, and carefully lifted Eric to her friend's breast. His crying stopped all at once as he latched on. Alice winced in pain.

'You okay?' said Beth. 'Want to stop?'

'No. He's just hungry.'

The sudden quiet was unnerving. Wind whispered eerily through the corridors, and Beth thought she heard a twig snapping. She glanced around, but they were alone.

You're surrounded by woodland. Sometimes twigs just...snap. Welcome to nature.

Something wet dripped onto her hand. It was one of Alice's tears. She gazed at Eric, greedily guzzling his milk.

'What's it like?' said Beth.

Alice sniffed away a string of blood-flecked mucus. 'What's what like?'

'You know. Having a baby.'

Alice almost smiled. 'It's hard. It's fucking hard. You can prepare yourself all you want, read all the books, go to the classes...but you're never ready. Your whole life changes, in good and bad ways, but after a while, you realise the shit you were afraid of is mostly pretty trivial. Mopping up sick, changing dirty nappies...it's nothing.'

'That doesn't sound too bad, I guess.'

Alice nodded. Eric had calmed, the initial struggle to latch on slowing to a gentler pace. 'That's not the worst, though. The real bad stuff is all the new worries. Like, why is he crying again? And if he's not, you think, why is he *not* crying? Is everything okay? Is he breathing? But then there're the good things. I can look at him, hold his little hand in mine, and know that I created that. He's part of me. And sure, he'll probably grow up to be embarrassed by me and eventually hate me, but for now he's mine and I love him, Beth. I love him so much I can't even—'

'I'm sorry,' said Beth abruptly. Alice looked up from her baby, looked her friend right in the eyes.

'For what?'

'For being a shitty friend.'

'Beth, you've—'

'No, I have. Back in the car, you were right. I've not been round to see you, and sometimes...sometimes I wish things were how they used to be.'

'Hey,' said Alice, 'it's okay. You don't like babies. You told me before.'

'And you said the same thing,' smiled Beth.

'I did. And at the time, I meant it. But just because I'm a mum now, it doesn't mean we can't still be best friends.'

'Don't take this the wrong way,' said Beth suddenly, as if she had to get it out, 'but part of me hates you.'

Alice didn't reply, and Beth continued.

'I mean, I love you, y'know, but I hate you too. Because you have something I don't. You have something to live for. I thought I did, once, but I didn't. I never have. It's funny. My boyfriend died, and my parents, and...I'm not even sure I care. It's made no difference to me. You'd think I'd feel empty inside, lost...but I already did. I've felt like that for a long time. I was born here, and I'm gonna die here. I've always known.'

'I'm the one who should be sorry,' said Alice.

'What for?'

'It's all my fault.'

Beth shook her head. 'Bollocks it is.'

'She's come for my baby. It's no coincidence, is it? The first baby in Auchenmullan for Christ knows how long, and she comes back...'

'We don't know that.'

They both did. There was no denying it. Beth's eyes roamed the walls, taking in the graffiti, the chipped plaster-board, the snow and leaf-covered floor. She felt curiously peaceful.

'He's done,' said Alice. Beth lowered Eric, resting him on her knees. He cooed sweetly, his big eyes struggling to stay open.

'Beth...promise me something.'

'Anything,' she said, buttoning up Alice's dress.

Alice leaned her head back. 'Promise me you'll take care of him. That you'll keep him safe, if I don't make it.'

'Don't talk like that.'

'Beth, *promise* me. I can't keep up, not with these fucking handcuffs on. If it comes down to it, promise you'll take Eric with you. That you'll protect him.'

'It won't come to that. We're in a sawmill, for fuck's sake, there'll be something to get those cuffs off.'

'There're no tools left. Steve stole the last chainsaw years ago.'

Beth remembered. Steve had draped some ham from his sandwich over his face and chased them around the mill with the chainsaw, shouting about being Leatherface and threatening to saw the girls' clothes off. The game had stopped when he had slipped on some cow shit and almost cut his own head off with the spinning blade.

'We'll find something,' said Beth, convincing neither of them.

Alice looked deep into her eyes. 'Promise me you'll take care of him.'

But Beth wasn't listening. She was watching the wall next to Alice's head.

It was bulging, *cracking*, and then it split wide open and a burnt hand emerged, reaching for them.

She was here.

Maggie had found them, and now they were going to die.

29

BETH LEAPT BACKWARDS, STILL CRADLING ERIC, AS THE HAND clamped shut over Alice's face.

She laid him down and dived for her friend, closing both hands over Maggie's gnarled fingers, using all her strength to try to prise them off. Maggie's nails dug into the pliant flesh of Alice's cheeks, rending them, the skin offering no resistance. Beth focused her attention on one long finger and bent it backwards. It snapped like dry kindling and she tossed it aside. She tried the next finger, as the claws drew deep bloody chasms across Alice's face, her screams muffled and indistinct.

Maggie withdrew, the hand vanishing back through the wall, and Alice toppled onto her side, blood squirting wildly from her ruptured flesh. Four scars lined her cheek, the longest reaching all the way from her eyeball to the corner of her mouth.

'Get up,' shouted Beth, trying to rouse her, to get her to stand, but she was a broken marionette, her limbs loose and tumbling. Beth looked to the hole in the wall, Maggie staring back at her, one pale grey eye pressed against it like a peeper spying on the girls' locker room.

'My...baby,' she said.

Through the ruin of her mouth, Alice managed to utter one word.

It sounded like, 'Go!'

Beth grabbed Eric and scrambled to her feet. His swaddling was wet from lying in the snow, and as she ran, he began to cry. She reached a door and barged into it, but a woodpile had collapsed on the other side, and the door would only open a couple of inches.

'Shit,' she said, refusing to let the horrifying reality that she was about to die take hold. She continued down the corridor, snow pouring in above her.

A fallen barrel vomited wood chips at her feet, and she hopped over it, heading for the next doorway. This one opened, but inside was nothing but a small office. There was a desk and the remains of a chair, and shattered glass sparkling in the moonlight, but no escape route.

A wall crumbled behind her.

Maggie, breaking through. She must be close.

Eric wailed and cried for his mother.

'Shut up,' said Beth. 'Please...she'll *hear* you!'

She knew he couldn't understand. He was two months old, for fuck's sake. She looked down at his tiny tear-streaked face, and he gazed up at her, his cries turning to pathetic sniffles.

She thought of Alice's last wish.

Promise me you'll take care of him.

It wasn't fair of her to ask. Beth could hardly take care of herself, never mind a baby. What could she do? They were going to die here. Alice was surely already dead, like all the rest of them.

It was just her left alive. Her and Eric.

You know what to do, said the voice. *End it. Survive. Give her the baby.*

She gazed down into his big green eyes. They reminded her of Alice's.

He's part of me, she had said.

Was that true?

Biologically speaking, she supposed it was. Eric was all that remained of Alice and Auchenmullan. She had failed to save Grady. She had failed to save Alice.

If she could protect Eric, then at least she would die knowing she had done something worthwhile in her miserable, sad little life.

The door at the end of the corridor had a ripped and faded warning sign on it. PROTECTIVE CLOTHING MUST BE WORN BEYOND THIS POINT, it read.

The main body of the mill lay behind that door. The layout was coming back to her in fits and starts, the fog of confusion slowly lifting. She ran down the corridor and entered, stepping into the room where she would make her final stand.

It was bigger than she remembered.

Enormous machines lined the floor like a robot graveyard, rusted and decaying. Two steel staircases at opposite ends of the room led to a gangway high above, the narrow walkway leaning against a giant woodchipper. She wondered briefly if she could knock Maggie into the machine, but that was dumb. There was no power anymore. Maggie would just climb back out again.

Tools lay scattered, but she didn't stop to pick one up. What use would a chisel or a mallet be against a witch? Plus, she needed both hands for Eric, the fat little bastard.

She heard footsteps, the soft crunch of snow beneath

stealthy feet, and nails scratching channels along rotted, damp walls. Time was almost up. In the corner of the room were two enormous furnaces that looked like they had sat there for centuries, their fires long-dimmed. She hurried over to them. The furnace doors were sealed shut with rust and filth. Beth laid Eric on the snow and took hold of the handle, the metal so cold it scalded her unprotected palms.

She pulled, but the damned thing wouldn't budge.

Gritting her teeth, she tried again, pushing off against the furnace with her foot. It creaked, it groaned...but it didn't open.

She gave up and moved on to the second — and final — furnace.

'Please,' she begged, tears in her eyes, as she took the handle and yanked hard. She needn't have bothered. The door swung open easily, and she almost yelped with joy. The interior was cavernous, thick with cobwebs and — she grimaced — rotting animal carcasses. It looked and smelled like a serial killer's basement, but this was not the time to complain.

Leave a review on Airbnb later, she thought, and hiccuped out a strained laugh.

She grabbed Eric, brushed off the snow, and placed him in the furnace. 'I'm sorry,' she said, as tears glistened on his pink cheeks. 'I'll come back for you.' She hesitated a moment, and said, 'I promise.'

Then came the worst part. She took the door in her trembling hands and closed it on the child. The door slammed shut, muting his cries. She felt like she was sealing him in a tomb.

He'll be fine, she told herself. *It's a big chimney. He can breathe in there.*

Every instinct urged her to wrench the door open and

free him, but the twisted part of her mind knew he was safer in there.

'*My...baby.*'

Beth whirled round, and there was Maggie, stooping to enter through the doorway. There was something different about her. The fire that had cloaked her had finally been extinguished, and she was moving slower, her steps laboured. Beth could see the ravages of the flames on Maggie's scrawny body. Her skin had darkened and crisped like fat on an overdone steak, and it fell in flakes with each tortuous step. Shards of mud-brown bone pierced through the aged flesh as she shuddered arthritically towards Beth. The only part that seemed unharmed was the yawning hole in her belly, the bright red insides pulsating rhythmically, the never-ending torrent of fresh blood gushing forth.

Beth remembered something Grady used to say.

'*If it bleeds, we can kill it.*'

Steve would always laugh and high-five him when he said that stupid phrase. She thought it was a quote from a movie, but didn't know which one, and didn't fucking care.

The time for thinking was over.

It was time to fight...or die.

'Come on then,' snarled Beth, as she locked eyes with Maggie from across the room. The witch smiled at her and creaked forward on withered legs.

Beth needed a weapon, or some kind of advantage. There were bricks and chunks of fallen masonry, a few hard-hats, even an old boot...but nothing she could defend herself with.

Or kill with, she reminded herself.

Her eyes travelled up one of the rickety-looking metal staircases. The thin walkway hung suspended from beams that once held the roof together. The few that remained were as charred and burnt as Maggie herself. Would they hold her weight?

Fuck, it wasn't like she had a choice. She rushed forwards and stepped onto the stairs. They wobbled from side-to-side, the corroded metal buckling underfoot.

'This is a bad idea,' she kept repeating, but she knew what was up there, and she needed it.

She recalled that night, in the early days of Auchenmullan's slide into nothingness, when Angus Muir had found his dad's hidden stash of vodka and porno mags, and brought two bottles and some magazines to the mill for everyone to gawk over.

Beth still remembered with shocking clarity the moment that he and Steve had raced up the stairs to the walkway, starting from opposite ends.

She remembered the way the metal had swayed, how Alice had taken her hand, how Grady had shouted at them to stop before someone got hurt.

And she remembered the step beneath Angus giving way as he approached the top, the way his body had twisted as he fell, and the sound of his skull splitting as he hit the floor.

She remembered all that, yet still she climbed.

For she knew that at the top of the staircase, halfway along the gangway, was a glass-panelled fire-safety box.

And within *that* was a fire axe.

No one — not even Steve — had been stupid enough to climb the stairs after Angus's accident. Even now, as Beth made her way falteringly up the steps, the staircase rocked menacingly.

At the other end of the room, Maggie placed her foot on the first step. The metal groaned, but she never noticed. She simply smiled, spread her long fingers wide, and gripped the rail.

The structure trembled as the women climbed, both heading for the walkway.

'Give...me...my...baby,' wheezed Maggie.

She was visibly weaker. Even her smile looked tired, and it made Beth think she might have a chance.

Is false hope better than no hope?

She was almost at the top when she reached the broken step where Angus had fallen. There, she made the mistake of looking down. The ground was far away, and she thought that, beneath the snow, she could still make out the bloodstain from where he had landed. Clinging to the rusted railing, she stepped over the gap and kept going, ready to face her destiny.

Don't look down again.

She couldn't allow herself to. Fear was a weakness the witch surely didn't possess, and if Beth was to get through this alive, and save Eric, she would need to overcome her *own* fears. The fire safety box was in sight, and she quickened her pace. The walkway moaned beneath her, the metal bending and howling.

She grabbed the rail for balance, and it snapped.

It fell from her hand, clattering to the ground thirty feet below. For one nightmarish second Beth thought she would follow, pinwheeling her arms in a panic. She threw herself backwards, her spine crunching against the other rail, and fell limp across the walkway.

Ohmygod ohmygod ohmygod.

Terror gripped her by the throat, her stomach tying itself in knots, muscles tightening. Doubt wormed its way into her mind. What the hell was she doing up here? Who was she kidding, thinking she could take on Maggie Wall, scourge of

Auchenmullan? She looked up and saw Maggie climbing the stairs. Another couple of steps and she'd reach the walkway.

Tell her where the baby is. Tell her and she'll let you live!

Beth's eyes blinked rapidly, her fingers twitching. She was losing it. How could she even think that? She had made a promise to her friend. Her best friend, a girl who was lying mauled somewhere nearby, torn to pieces by Maggie.

'Fuck off,' she sobbed. 'Leave us alone and *fuck off.*'

She couldn't get up.

The moon dipped behind a cloud, and the mill fell into unfathomable darkness as Beth lay prone on the walkway. She could taste vomit in her mouth and hear Maggie's footsteps.

The cloud passed, moonlight flooding in again. Maggie was close. She was almost level with the fire axe.

Beth couldn't allow that to happen.

Maggie had taken everything from her. Her friends, her family...perhaps even her sanity. All gone, in the blink of a witch's eye. Only one thing remained. A promise she had made. A promise that she had to keep.

It wasn't much, but it was enough.

Beth clung to the railing, forcing herself to stand, fighting against the anxiety that wracked her body, that made her sweat, made her tremble, made her lose control of her bladder. The walkway oscillated to-and-fro, the beams above her rasping under the strain.

Maggie drew nearer, the deluge from her belly drenching the frail metal and splattering noisily on the floor far beneath them.

Beth let go of the rail and walked towards her, fists clenched.

'Come on, you bitch,' she muttered, unaware she was

doing so. She broke into a run. The structure wobbled, and even Maggie paused. Her grin contorted into a trepidatious leer.

Beth reached the metal box and dropped to her knees, slamming her elbow into the glass front, breaking it into long shards.

Maggie was so close that Beth could smell her. The odour, like burning marshmallows over a campfire, was not unpleasant. She reached into the kit, her fingers closing around the handle of the axe.

'My...baby,' said Maggie.

'No way,' said Beth, tearing the axe from the box and brandishing it with both hands. God, it was heavy! She rested it on the railing as she faced down Maggie Wall.

'I saw what they did to you,' she said. 'And I'm sorry. But this has to end.'

Maggie paused, looking at her through bleary eyes.

'Took...my...baby,' she said.

'I know,' sobbed Beth, her voice teetering on the brink of insanity. 'They had no right. You were no witch. You were a woman. A mother. Just like my friend.'

She couldn't stop talking. What did she think she was going to do — reason with her?

Maggie stepped closer.

'You can't have him,' said Beth, tears rolling down her cheeks. 'I won't let you.'

'Mine,' said Maggie. 'All...mine.'

Maggie lunged forwards, arms grasping at thin air, but she was slow. This was not the same witch that had chased them down the mountain in a blur of frenzied motion. Every movement was an effort. Beth dodged her attack, drew the axe back, and swung. Maggie thrust her arm up, and the axe head sliced through her wrist, severing the hand with a dry pop. It fell to the walkway, and Maggie took a step back, hissing venom.

The fingers on the severed appendage wriggled, and Beth stomped her heel down, grinding the hand to ash. Maggie's ghoulish grin slipped from her face, her eyes burning with uncontrolled fury. She lashed out again, catching Beth off-guard, the claws of her remaining hand gouging flesh from Beth's arm.

Beth screamed in pain and buried the axe in Maggie's side. The witch barely reacted, the weapon sliding out. Blood soaked the sleeve of Beth's jacket, spilling down her arm.

From below, Eric's screams reached a fever pitch, audible even through the thick door of the furnace.

Maggie licked a ragged tongue over her teeth, her smile returning. She glared at Beth.

'My...baby.'

'Leave him alone!'

Beth brandished the axe, her own blood hot against her skin, and came at the witch, chopping wildly, ferociously. The axe head slammed into Maggie's breast, and the creature — that once, many years ago, had been a young woman named Maggie Wall — recoiled from the blow.

'I've got you, you old bitch,' roared Beth.

She yanked the axe free, then brought it down again, this time on Maggie's neck. Maggie screamed, an ear-piercing lamentation, and instinctively covered her swollen, gaping belly with what remained of her arms.

Beth hacked at them, adrenaline flowing through her. Maggie tried to protect herself, but Beth came at her in a burst of cold-blooded strength, and the witch backed off, suddenly fearful.

The walkway gave way beneath her, and Maggie's leg

plunged through the gap, the sharp edges stabbing into her bark-like thigh, the dried skin crumbling.

The structure shook. Something cracked above them, and one of the remaining roof beams hurtled through the air and crashed to the floor.

Beth knew the whole place was gonna fall, but she didn't care.

She brought the axe down. It split Maggie's skull, cleaving it open, revealing a dried-up, sponge-like brain, but Beth was not finished. Again and again she hacked at Maggie like a crazed lumberjack, the axe head thudding off her unprotected body, carving a relentless pattern into her trunk. High up, another beam snapped and fell from the sky, and the walkway tilted at an obscene angle.

Beneath the celestial glare of the full, fat moon, and with soft snow whirling dreamlike before her eyes, Beth swung the axe one last time.

As she did so, she thought about all the bad choices she had made throughout her life, and was surprised to find she regretted none of them.

The axe embedded itself in the wound in Maggie's belly.

Blood thundered out like a geyser, the spray battering Beth in the face, almost knocking her off her feet. She released the axe and staggered away, forced backwards by the crimson torrent. Her hip hit the railing and over she went, trying desperately to grasp the metal with her trailing hand. Her fingers closed around it, but they were wet with blood.

Beth sailed weightlessly through the air for what seemed an eternity, so long she thought she may never land, blood raining down all around her, a curious red waterfall. She thought of Eric, and Alice, and smiled at how she had done her friend proud, and then—

Snap!

She came down hard on her ankle, the bone fracturing and tearing through her skin. The rest of her followed, hitting the ground hard.

As she lay there, the walkway shook, broke, and collapsed to the ground in a tangle of warped metal, depositing Maggie onto the snow-covered floor of the old saw mill. She landed on her stomach with a thump, the axe bursting through her back, sending more fountains of crimson gore spurting into the air, and turning the lily-white snow as red as the devil himself.

THE STARS WERE ESPECIALLY BRIGHT TONIGHT.

Beth looked up at them and wept, the falling snowflakes melting on her cheeks.

She let her head loll to the side, looking at the ragged body of Maggie Wall as it entered its death throes. The crazed fountain still spurted, but it was no longer as strong. It slowed to a trickle, and then — the way all things must — to nothing.

When Beth awoke, it had stopped snowing, and the sun hinted over the roofless walls of the mill.

She forced herself to sit. The blood that coated her body had dried, and she inspected her ankle. The bone jutted out from her leg, her foot facing the wrong way entirely, but she felt no pain.

She felt nothing at all.

There was no relief, no joy in victory...for it had come at a grim price.

Her parents were dead. Her friends, too. Alice, Grady, Steve...gone, all gone.

Maggie lay beneath the collapsed walkway, still and lifeless. Beth had expected her body to have vanished, or been dragged down to hell, or something equally supernatural. But no, she just lay there like a fallen tree after a storm. It was oddly prosaic, all things considered.

She crawled over to Maggie to inspect the remains, dragging her broken foot behind her. The witch had petrified overnight, her body frozen and black like a frostbitten toe, a rictus grin still plastered on her squat little face. Beth ran her hand across the hard skin of Maggie's cheek.

'I'm sorry,' she said, and she meant it.

It wasn't Maggie's fault. *They* had done this to her, all those centuries ago. The people of Auchenmullan.

The real monsters.

She pictured their faces, that group of frightened, powerless men hiding behind their swords and crucifixes, so scared and impotent. Perhaps she was even a descendant of one of them. Her mother's family had always lived in the Highlands. Who knew how far back the Malone dynasty stretched?

A tear fell, landing on Maggie's face, disappearing into the firm, porous skin.

All she wanted was her baby. Was that too much to ask?

Her baby.

A bleak chill traced Beth's spine.

Where *was* Eric?

She had forgotten all about him. She laughed. Oh, she knew she shouldn't...but still she laughed. All that she had gone through to protect him...and for a moment, she had forgotten he even existed.

'I'd be a terrible mother,' she said, and laughed even harder.

She wondered if she was losing her mind.

Nonsense, she thought. *You've already lost it. It happened right around the time you split open a three-hundred-year-old witch's skull with an axe.*

'That oughta do it,' she murmured.

She looked to the furnaces. One of the doors was ajar. That was funny. She certainly hadn't left it like that.

Maybe Eric got bored and went for a walk?

She laughed at that too. Laughter came easy to her now that everyone she loved was dead.

She leaned over and kissed the witch on her pruned forehead.

'Goodbye, Maggie,' she said, and she could have sworn the corners of the witch's mouth curled slightly.

My...baby...

That voice...was it in her head? Beth thought so, and didn't care either way. Let them talk. There was no one left for her to speak to, anyway.

She pulled the axe from Maggie's dried-up husk, using it for balance as she hobbled towards the furnace.

Poor Maggie, she kept thinking. *Poor, poor Maggie.*

She was dead too, and Beth had killed her. It had been the right thing to do. If not, then Maggie would have killed *her*. It was survival. That was the only thing that mattered.

Survival.

As she shambled towards the furnaces, she couldn't help wondering how much better would things have been had they just given Maggie the baby?

My...baby...

'Yes, Maggie,' she said. *'Your baby.'*

Would everyone still be alive? Was Eric's life worth dozens of others? To Alice, yes. But to Beth, Eric had robbed her of everything she held dear. What right did Alice have to ask her to look after him? It was like a punishment from beyond the grave.

She should have asked Maggie. She would have been happy to take him.

By the time Beth reached the furnace, the sun was nearly up and the birds were singing in the crisp ruby sky. A glorious new day had arrived.

She looked inside, and Eric was gone.

'Huh,' she said, and laughed again. It was an unnatural sound, and it scared her.

'Beth,' said a garbled voice from behind.

Maggie?

Beth turned, smiling. At the sight of Alice and Eric, the smile faded.

Alice sat against the wall, a portrait of torment, her face a death-mask of pure white skin and scarlet-streaked gore. On her lap lay Eric.

'Is he...'

'He's fine,' said Alice. The handcuffs dangled from one wrist, and the thumb on her other hand was missing, a bloodied, ragged stump in its place. A trail of blood led from Alice to a worktable by the wall, and the bloodstained vice attached to it. A small stub of flesh and bone poked out between the metal slabs.

Alice must have crushed her own thumb to a pulp to free herself. It was an impressive display, though not nearly as impressive as rising from the grave and destroying a town. Beth choked back a giggle.

It didn't seem appropriate.

Pull yourself together.

Alice just sat there, her face a shredded mess, dried blood congealing around the wounds and staining her dress. For a long time, neither of them said a word, until Alice broke the silence.

'Thank you,' she said, as best as her damaged mouth would allow.

Beth just nodded. There were no words.

Alice was still alive, and so was Eric. They were together, reunited, a happy little family.

Beth knew she should be ecstatic...but still she felt nothing. Well, that wasn't quite true. She felt a deep, simmering resentment.

'You saved Eric,' mumbled Alice. 'You'll never know how much—'

'It's okay,' said Beth.

My...baby...

That voice...it was definitely in her head, right?

Right?

She glanced over at Maggie, feeling a strange kinship with her. Two lost souls, forever searching for something, a reason to live, a reason to exist. Alice had Eric, Maggie *wanted* Eric, and Beth had nothing.

It wasn't fair.

'I thought you were dead,' she said.

'So did I,' said Alice, air spitting out through the ravages in her cheeks. If she had picked up on the malice in Beth's statement, she didn't show it.

Why would she? All she cares about is that fucking baby. She doesn't care about you. She never did. She used you.

That wasn't true...it *couldn't* be true.

My...baby...

Every bone in her body throbbed, and the sun burned her eyes.

'Is she dead?' said Alice.

'I don't think so,' she said, and laughed one final time.

Alice looked up at her with panic in her eyes. 'What?'

But the Beth that she knew was no longer there. She stood watching as Maggie's dry bones rattled and smouldered, the black, hardened shell of her body splitting and cracking.

'She just wanted her baby,' said Beth. She wiped away a tear. 'That's all she wanted.'

'You have to get Eric out of here,' said Alice, sounding exhausted.

The red blood that had frozen around Maggie started to thaw, but Alice hadn't noticed.

She's so wrapped up in her little bubble, so focused on herself and Eric, that she's blind to everything around her.

Did she really expect Beth to go head-to-head with Maggie again? Was that all she was to Alice, her fucking bodyguard? She had chopped up a witch with an axe like some lunatic escapee from a fairy tale...did she not deserve a fucking rest?

'Guess I'm expendable,' muttered Beth, as Maggie's blood flowed back along the melting snow, heading towards her desiccated corpse.

She couldn't do it again. She couldn't fight Maggie a second time.

Hell, she *wouldn't* do it.

Maggie's arm twitched, and Beth knew what she needed to do. Something that should have been done *long* before now. It was all so simple.

'Beth, *please,*' said Alice.

She turned to Alice. 'What more do you want from me?'

'Beth...'

'Haven't I done enough?'

It wasn't fair. Alice had caused this. Alice and Eric.

'It's your fault,' said Beth. *'You have her baby.'*

Maggie's head slowly rotated. Her mouth widened into a grin. The burnt flesh on her body cracked open, leathery-grey limbs emerging like a snake shedding its skin. She rose, back-lit by the hazy red glow of the morning sun. Beth thought it was the most beautiful thing she'd ever seen.

'Beth, that's not you talking. It's not you.'

'She'll never stop,' she said. 'She'll just keep coming, forever and ever.'

Alice finally spotted Maggie. She tried to scream, succeeding only in tearing her facial scars open again.

'Don't you see, Al? We'll never be free. You, me, Maggie...we'll never be free.'

Alice stared at her, horrified, and Beth chuckled sadly.

'Just do it,' she said. 'Just give it to her. *She's never going to stop.*'

'You're insane,' said Alice, attempting to shuffle away. Beth grabbed the hem of her dress and pulled her back.

'Give her the baby. Give it to her. Just do it, give her the baby.' She was babbling now. 'Come on, hand it over. She'll stop once she has it. She'll leave us alone. Don't you see? It's the only way!'

'He's not an *it*,' said Alice. 'He's my son.'

'He belongs to Maggie!' shouted Beth. She reached for Eric, took a handful of his swaddling and pulled. He wailed, and Beth hit him across the face.

'Stop!' screamed Alice. She tried to push Beth away with her damaged hand, but Beth grabbed it and squeezed down on the stump. Alice roared in pain, and Beth yanked harder on Eric, her eyes wide and manic.

'Give her the fucking baby! She'll let us live, you selfish bitch!'

But Alice wouldn't let her. She clung to her son, curling her body protectively around him.

'Give her the baby! Give it to her or I'll fucking kill you!'

Beth glanced round and saw Maggie advancing. She looked exactly as she had the night before, fresh out of the grave, only this time she was unhurried.

Beth pummelled her best friend, sitting over her, battering her soft body. She pulled out a clump of Alice's hair, then hooked two fingers into the scars on her cheek and ripped them wide open. She rolled Alice onto her back, smacking her across her torn, bleeding face.

'It's him or me! Don't you fucking understand? It'll never end!' She shook Alice, took her head in both hands, and slammed it off the floor. *'It's just one baby, you selfish fucking cunt!'*

Alice's head cracked against the concrete, once, twice, three times, her eyes taking on a glazed look. As they partially closed — and Beth stole Eric from her limp hands — Alice managed two words.

'You...promised.'

Beth looked at her for a moment, holding Eric away from her body as if afraid to touch him.

'I'm not sorry,' she said, and it was the truth. When she looked down at Alice, all she saw was a woman who wanted her to die, to give up her life for someone she had only met twice, a child for whom death held no meaning.

She could always have another one.

Beth turned to Maggie, holding the wailing infant out to her like a macabre offering.

'Here's your baby!' she said. 'Take it...take it and go home.'

Maggie reached out, head swaying, wrapping her foul hands around the bundle. Up close, Beth could see insects crawling over Maggie's skin, her body alive with unnatural wildlife.

Maggie gazed lovingly upon the child as Beth limped backwards, the pain of her broken ankle little more than an inconvenience.

'Take it,' said Beth, 'and go. Just let me live. Please.'

She turned to Alice, saw her watching through half-lidded eyes, and looked away. The strange, wicked voice in her head had fallen silent.

'I'm not sorry,' she said again, as Maggie held Eric in one

outstretched hand and tenderly unwrapped his swaddling with the other. He was quiet, looking up at Maggie with rapt attention. She smiled at him, running her foul tongue over her lips, and he giggled with delight.

Then Maggie's smile faltered. She turned to Beth.

'Not...my...baby,' she said.

'What do you mean? *That's your fucking baby right there, you dumb bitch!*'

Maggie ran a spindly finger down Eric's face and gently placed him on the ground with the loving touch of a mother.

Beth backed away as Maggie took a step towards her.

'What are you doing?' she roared. 'I gave you the baby! *I gave you the fucking baby! That's what you wanted!*'

Beth put all her weight on her left leg, forgetting about her ankle until the pain erupted up her calf and she collapsed hard on the snowy floor.

'No,' said Maggie. 'Not...mine.'

She unfurled a crooked arm and grabbed Beth by her broken foot, dragging her across the ground, the bones in her ankle grinding together as the witch leered down at her. Maggie's face crumpled, the smile becoming a sneer, her eyes narrowing to angry slits.

'You...have...it,' she said.

'No! No, you're wrong! You're fucking wrong!'

What did she mean? She had given Maggie the baby! It was hers now!

Beth screamed as Maggie tore her jacket open and plunged the fingers of one hand into her abdomen. The other followed, pressing into the pale, doughy flesh of her belly, then in one almighty motion, Maggie ripped her stomach open, the two flaps slopping wetly to either side.

Hot blood gushed over the snow, and Beth cried, closing her eyes. She didn't need to see. She already knew.

If only she had realised sooner.

Decrepit hands brushed past her internal organs, catching on them, dragging them out of place. Blood gurgled in her throat and she started to choke.

Maggie removed her hands from Beth's stomach. She was holding something, something small.

As Beth died, she thought back to that night a few months ago when Grady's condom had broken, and how they had considered going to Inverness to get the morning-after pill, but both of them had been too hungover to drive. It was the last time they had fucked. Beth hadn't planned it, but she was drunk and horny, and Grady had been bugging her about it all evening.

She was still thinking of that moment when Maggie bit into the cord that connected Beth to the barely developed foetus.

'Mine,' said Maggie, as she held the tiny figure before her own belly. The great gaping wound in her stomach puckered and drooled in anticipation, and Maggie smiled.

Beth turned to Alice one last time and looked at her through eyes cloudy with tears.

Alice just sat there, watching.

No, thought Beth. Not just watching. Was Alice *laughing* at her?

As a matter of fact, she was.

DAWN BROKE OVER AUCHENMULLAN.

Police cars swarmed the landscape like ants. When PC Blackwood hadn't checked in, two more squad cars had been sent to investigate. And when the occupants of *those* vehicles discovered the unbridled carnage of Blackwood and his fellow officers, even more vehicles were despatched. The press, too, had gotten wind of the situation, although no one was quite prepared for the horror they would find in the town hall.

Bodies sliced, ripped, torn, mutilated, burnt, dismembered, eviscerated...not a soul was left alive.

Overnight, Auchenmullan had been wiped from the map.

The search was broadened to cover the whole town, in the hopes of finding at least one survivor. Peter Lamb's scattered limbs were discovered near the shoe tree, and at Spring-heeled Jack's Bowling Alley, the grisly remains of Jack dripped down the walls of the bathroom stall and pooled on the floor beneath a heap of steaming viscera.

At around four, as the sun set and darkness encroached,

a badly disfigured woman staggered into town carrying a baby.

She was near death, and suffering from hypothermia, her white dress wrapped around her infant son. Both were taken promptly to hospital, and both survived.

When Alice's bandages were removed and she was able to speak again, she told a story so fantastical that the officer taking her statement struggled to keep a straight face.

Alice learned never to tell the story again.

The doctors said she had suffered such a severe shock that she had invented an elaborate fantasy to make sense of it all. They told her a lot of things, and she nodded and agreed with them all.

In time, the doctors said, *your memory of the events may return. Until then, don't force it. These things take time.*

To this day, the case remains unsolved, and Alice Burman, who now lives on a busy residential street in Glasgow with her young son Eric, quietly hopes it will remain that way.

Around the time that Alice and Eric entered the devastated corpse of Auchenmullan, a similar homecoming was taking place several miles along the road and up the mountain, out toward Cook's Point.

There was no one around to see it.

No fanfare, no nosy journalists, no questioning police.

Just one woman coming home with her baby after a long and difficult night.

With the dappled sun on her back, Maggie Wall strode past her empty grave, stepping over the remains of the teenagers, and crossed the threshold into her cabin. She hadn't been here in a long, long time, but it was as she remembered. Her pot of soup still boiled over the open fire, and the sweet smell of chicken and herbs filled the air.

She sat there for hours, contented, as night drew its velvet cloak over the mountain. As Maggie Wall stared out across the valley, the flashing police lights in the distance gradually disappeared, leaving nothing but the sound of the wind whistling through the trees.

After a while, her baby started to cry.

Maggie smiled.

The little one was hungry.

AFTERWORD

Maggie's Grave is based on a true story. Well, sort of.

Her grave *does* exist.

You can find it in the small Scottish village of Dunning, in Perthshire. I took some serious liberties with it for the book, of course. In real life, it stands in a field by the side of the road, not at the top of a mountain, and it actually reads MAGGIE WALL BURNT HERE AS A WITCH, which I changed to MAGGIE WALL BURIED HERE AS A WITCH to suit the story.

The origins of the grave are something of a mystery. It's the only monument in the UK to be dedicated to a witch, and yet no trace of her can be found in the history books. The grave is still regularly tended to, but no one knows who by.

I visited with my wife back in 2014, and the grave has stuck with me all these years. There was certainly a sinister atmosphere around it, sitting there alone on a windswept field. There were various offerings tucked between the rocks, from flowers and ribbons to a plastic figure of Toad from Super Mario Brothers.

Perhaps we'll never get to the bottom of the real mystery behind Maggie's grave, but I don't think it matters. Some mysteries are better left unsolved...for the sake of all humanity.

As always, a big thanks to my wife Heather, who plastered and painted our entire living room while I sat finishing this book during lockdown. Love you!

Thanks to Boris the pug, who is a very good boy.

Big thanks to Trevor Henderson for his awesome cover, check out his work on Twitter!

Cheers to Johann and Emily and Steve and Brad and Andy for their excellent feedback and suggestions. Much appreciated!

And most of all, thanks once more to you, dear reader. These books wouldn't be here without your continued support. You're the best.

I normally leave you with my writing playlist, but it's a bit difficult this time, because the music is not available on Spotify or iTunes. However, it is all available from Bandcamp, and you can choose how much you pay for each album. I mean look, it's possible to download every album on here for free, but please support the artist and pay what you can afford. The music is chilling folk-horror soundtrack at its finest.

Go to https://klausmorlock.bandcamp.com to find all of the following records.

Klaus Morlock — *The Bridmore Lodge Tapes*
Klaus Morlock — *The Child Garden*
Klaus Morlock — *Bethany's Cradle*
Klaus Morlock — *Penumbra*
Klaus Morlock — *Old Negatives*
Klaus Morlock — *The Three Faces of Janice*
Klaus Morlock — *Dead Maids Assembly*
Klaus Morlock — *The Hermit of Lake Lugano*
Klaus Morlock — *Lost Valley VHS*
Klaus Morlock and the Tape Circle — *Klaus Morlock and the Tape Circle*
The Unseen — *The Blackheath Tapes*
The Unseen — *The Goatman*

ABOUT THE AUTHOR

David Sodergren lives in Scotland with his wife Heather and
his best friend, Boris the Pug. Growing up, he was the kind
of kid who collected rubber skeletons and lived for horror
movies.
Not much has changed since then.
His first novel, The Forgotten Island, was published in 2018.
This was followed by Night Shoot, a brutal throwback to the
early 80s slasher movie cycle, in 2019.
2020 is Sodergren's biggest year yet, with two new horror
novels being published — the slasher-noir Dead Girl Blues,
and the blood-soaked folk-horror Maggie's Grave.

Find David at the following locations —

https://paperbacksandpugs.wordpress.com
https://twitter.com/paperbacksnpugs
https://www.instagram.com/paperbacksandpugs/

Printed in Great Britain
by Amazon

43678966R00152